A Manic Kind of Love

By

Colleen Michaels

TOTAL
PUBLISHING
& MEDIA

www.TotalPublishingAndMedia.com

ISBN: 978-1-936750-35-1

Dedication

W hen I was in my early 20s, everything seemed temporary to me. My family had moved around a lot during my childhood years, so friends would come and go from my life like sneakers. The constant flux that was my life also found its way into my relationships. I never expected to be with anybody for more than a few months. The idea of loving somebody for the rest of my life was something out of a Disney movie and nothing more.

But one couple changed my whole outlook on love and committing to one person for the rest of my life. It happened while I worked at a hotel in college. There was an elderly couple who would come in from time-to-time and stay in our best suite. I couldn't tell you their last names, but I will never forget how they held hands whenever they walked together. He was always there to open a door for her and he always had a smile on his face when he looked at her.

One day, the elderly gentleman came down to the front desk and we spoke about love for a few minutes. He said they'd been married for 35 years. The two of them had known each other since high school and randomly met up years later after their individual divorces. He said they reconnected quickly and were married within a year.

I asked him what the key was to finding true love. I will never forget the smile he had on his face while answering such a powerful question to somebody so young. He told me his wife drives him crazy every single day of his life. He paused and then said but she seldom makes him mad. You see, he wasn't insulting his wife. Instead, he meant that every time he looked at her, heard her voice or held her hand, he fell in love with her all over again.

This book is dedicated to the journey of finding your best friend, your true love, and a happily ever after. I know it's out there, because I've witnessed it in person.

Table of Contents

Chapter 1—Suicides are Never Clean 1

Chapter 2—Sex . . . . Crying . . . . and
a Hot Shower...................................... 10

Chapter 3—Here Comes the Bride 21

Chapter 4—A Tricky Little Dance 35

Chapter 5—Making Popcorn . . . . Not Love.............. 40

Chapter 6—Flipping the Perception Switch 50

Chapter 7—Drinking . . . . a Good Friend . . . . and
Morning Surprises............................... 61

Chapter 8—Our First Date.. 72

Chapter 9—The Asshole Strikes Back 84

Chapter 10—Asking Her to Go Steady 96

Chapter 11—One Happy Fucking Family 106

Chapter 12—I'll Take a Woman Scorned to Go 115

Chapter 13—I'm too Old for Break-ups 125

Chapter 14—Finding Out What Truly Matters......... 133

Chapter 15—A Stout Love Never Dies 143

Chapter 16—Wooing My Love Back
                    Into My Arms.................................... 152

Chapter 17—The Day I Fell to One Knee 162

Chapter 18—Celebrating Our Engagement under
                    the Wrong Lights 172

Chapter 19—It's Never Too Late.............................. 182

Chapter 20—Happily Ever After With
                    My Best Friend 195

Epilogue 204

Chapter 1

Suicides are Never Clean

It's funny how the air always seems cooler on suicide calls. Whether it's a mansion in South Tulsa or a shit-hole apartment up town, the end result is always the same: a person needed rescuing and nobody was there to lend a hand.

Readers, this is where my little tale to you begins. My partner and I were headed to a DOA call in the wealthy suburbs. It's one of the more surreal experiences an EMS worker will have. George and I will walk into a home neither of us will ever be able to afford, walk over to a body that has a bullet in it or a rope burn on the throat, and we will declare this poor soul to be deceased.

We pulled up to the home and everything seemed so calm. The house is a cookie cutter of every other mansion on the street. There is a basketball pole, a heated pool and a garden fit for the White House. The garage is big enough for three luxury vehicles and a palm tree or two.

George and I have a routine for DOA missions. Yes, it might seem a little crude to the outside observer, but sanity is sometimes more important than manners. George pulls out a tiny cigar and I pull out a Camel. We sit in the cab of our truck, roll down the windows and take our time puffing in the misery of our own lives. Non-smokers always assume the only reason I smoke is because I'm addicted to the nicotine—and they would be only half right. For me, it's about having one thing in my life that I can count on to make me happy. Each day, I can afford to smoke 10 cigarettes, and at three minutes a piece, I'm guaranteed at least thirty minutes a day of relaxation. Sure, this shit will kill me one day. If I didn't know any better, I would quit now and take up gum chewing or jogging. But I work in a business where death is common and most of the time nobody gets to decided how we die. So fuck my lungs! Fuck cigarettes! And fuck cancer! Chances are I'll probably get hit by a bus or fall prey to my cat allergies long before cigarettes do me in, anyways.

George and I decided it was time to head towards death. The walk towards the house is always the same. Neighbors are gawking at us through their windows. Dogs are barking in the distance. But mostly, everything is quiet and in slow motion as we work our way through the white picket fence and toward the inevitable.

When we reached the door, lights could be seen inside the house and sobbing could be heard. Please don't let this be a house full of hysterical people! There is nothing worse than trying to do your job and having a crying family member hanging on your leg; like a two-year-old needing attention or apple juice. I just wanted to tell those people to go into shock and shut the hell up!

It was game time and I needed to get my 'I give a fuck'-look on my face. You see, at that point I didn't give a fuck. Nobody special seemed to care about me and my empathy for others was pretty non-existent.

I always let George take the lead on these calls. He was about to knock on the door probably made from the tree found only in a dying rain forest, when a sobbing female invited us inside.

"Where is he?" George asked the grieving female.

The female pointed upstairs and then dropped to her knees crying. Fuck. I had just smoked and now there was stairs and heavy equipment to carry. I wonder if my DVR is recording the Sooners game right now? Oh, a burger sounds good when we get done from here.

George entered the room first. Right on cue, I started to feel the air getting cold. I looked to my left . . . .

"He's very dead," I said.

The poor fucker had shot himself with his handgun. Bits and pieces of him were spread out over his desk and chair. What a shame. That chair had cup holders and it appears to have massaging capabilities.

"Call it," I said, wondering if the burger joint just down the road would still be open after we're done with this guy.

"Time of death is eight," George said, quietly.

The cause of death was just another rich white man who was in over his head and chose the easy way out. Or maybe he's a gambler and just lost everything. Perhaps, his less than desirable wife stopped giving him the good loving and his mistress just wasn't enough not to shoot himself. Regardless of the cause, there was no open casket viewing for this poor asshole. I always wonder if suicide victims have to walk around with their wounds in the after-life?

"George, call for clean-up crew," I said, while wondering if onion rings would be a swell choice for a side with my burger. "I'll go down stairs and make sure the family stays away."

Now, my job sucks on many different levels, but at least I don't have to sit and console the family members. I leave that delectable duty to the fine men in blue. My job is to direct the cops in a coordinated fashion to keep the family members away from the dead body. . . . I mean their deceased kin. What bullshit. There is nothing upstairs, but a gun, a hot mess and letters trying to explain the insanity. That man's soul was no longer with us. Plus, the asshole got his blood on the suicide notes, so his family really wouldn't be able to read much of it anyways. Who writes notes these days? I always thought if I was going to off myself, there would be a website or a hot air balloon that declares to anybody who cares, that I . . . . of sound body and mind . . . . have killed myself and you should go back to your previously scheduled program. There should be no crying with my suicide. Instead, there should just be a moment of silence with James Earl Jones exclaiming, "That poor bastard." Readers, I thought I understood the pointlessness of suicides.

"Can you tell me why?" a girl said, she was in her 20s and had tears slowly running down her face. "You must see this kind of thing a lot?"

When a sexy girl asks me a question I'm always willing to answer.

"I am sorry for your loss," I said, with an idiot smile on my face. "I do see this a lot, but I really have no insight for you. I wish I did."

"You are so sweet," the female said, adjusting her body to show quite the stacked cleavage. "So, does your wife or girlfriend help you get through calls like tonight?"

Now, I know this girl and I had just met. You're probably thinking that I hate my job. I detest my life and swear like a sailor. Saying all of that, my job does afford me open access to vulnerable, sexy women who just want to fuck and get their minds off whatever bad thing just happened. I have fucked beautiful mothers, wives, sisters, aunts…hell; I even fucked a woman whose husband had just swallowed enough sleeping pills to put Charlie Sheen down for the count. Yes, I was a jerk and perhaps a little bit of a man whore now that I think about it.

"I'm not currently seeing anybody," I said with a coy grin on my face. "Do you have a man in your life?"

It didn't really matter how she answered the question. I would have bet anybody cash that I could still get her in the sack.

"No, not currently," she said, with a flirty smile now dominating her face. "My name is Amy."

Seriously, stop judging me about this woman. Why shouldn't I have taken this beautiful redhead home with me? She has legs for days and her breasts are begging for some motor boat action. Besides, I needed the distraction.

"Hey Ian," George said, grabbing me on my shoulder. "I think we're about done here."

George is not what you'd call a ladies man. In fact, the dude can be pretty oblivious when it comes to women. To be fair, he's divorced after being married for 15 years. The only things his wife left him were two kids, a beer gut, and the self-esteem of a chess player. Still, that man cock blocked me all of the time without any realization of his offenses.

"George, meet the beautiful Amy," I said, motioning to him with my eyes to get lost. "She and I were just talking."

"Well, I'm ready to go when you are Casanova," George said, with a smirk and a punch to my back. "If we hurry, we can still grab that burger."

"Are you leaving?" Amy said, with a worried, pouty look on her face.

"Do you want to come with?" I said, not expecting anything but a yes from Amy.

"Sure." she responded. "I would love to."

"No, you wouldn't," another female exclaimed, in a harsh voice coming from behind me.

I turned around expecting somebody's mother to be giving me the stink face. After all, how dare I try to pick up a grieving family member at the scene of a suicide? Instead, I found something completely different.

"You're doing this here?" The female said, in a very harsh tone.

"Liz, stop bothering the poor man," Amy said. "He's been nothing but sweet to me."

"Amy, Mom wants you in the kitchen," Liz said, while giving me a dirty, evil look. "Right now!"

Great, first it was my partner trying to prevent my evening fun and now it's the older, sexier, brunette sister. My first thought was to defend my actions. Obviously, she had just mistaken my intentions. I'm an honorable EMS worker, who was just trying to console the family member of a suicide victim. Yeah, she saw right through me.

"What an asshole," Liz said, while trying not to hit me. "Amy is barely 23 and her father just died and here you are trying to get in her pants. What an asshole."

"Ma'am, I was just doing my job," I said, with my best innocent look on my face. "How are you doing with this tragedy?"

Hind sight is 20/20, but that wasn't one of my better ideas. Liz's face began to get really red. I knew something bad was going to happen, but I got distracted by George's plea to leave. When I returned my attention toward Liz, she was now standing inches away from me.

"You know, I like to be dangerous too," she whispered, ever so gently into my ear.

"Ma'am, I think you have the wrong idea about me," I said, trembling from head to toe due to her soft breath brushing across my neck.

Unfortunately, or perhaps very fortunately, she wasn't buying what I was selling. Liz proceeded to run her soft, but cold hand across the back of my neck, lightly playing with my hair. She leaned in real close, almost as though she was going to kiss me in front of the 15 or so people grieving around the house.

"If you want to play . . . ." she said, with the voice of a siren. "Play with somebody your own age."

Every word that came out of her mouth gave my arms goose bumps. She made me so nervous that my mind started to escape me. Did I remember to feed my dog this morning? Did I have a dog? I needed to get a grip, but instead I dug myself into a deeper hole.

"Do you want to go somewhere?" I asked, hoping to Christ and my dick that this was about to happen.

Liz began to slowly move us toward the door. The whole time, she maintained close eye contact with me. This girl's blue eyes were intense to say the least. They seemed to have the uncanny power to destroy my defenses and put me at ease. While I did detect a certain amount of flirting coming from her eyes, there was definitely something missing. I just couldn't put my finger on what I was seeing.

We reached the door and Liz slowly opened it, while moving her hands down to my hips. Her face moved ever more closely to mine.

"You are an asshole," she said, so softly that I didn't make it out right away. "I'm not in the business of rewarding assholes."

Just like that, she pushed me outside and closed the door. I was left on the porch, with a hard on and sure that I had indeed owned a dog.

"Did you just get thrown out of the house?" George said with a snicker, while standing at our truck. "We still have time to go and grab that burger!"

I wasn't hungry anymore. Okay, that's bullshit. I was hungry, but for the beautiful, charismatic, intoxicating woman who had just stood up to me. No woman had ever done that to me before. Had she really just made me the prey in this hunt we call being single? Nah, her father just blew is brains out. That had to be the reason why she rejected me. I was sure my game had remained intact.

"George, let's go get that burger," I said, while overwhelmed with thoughts of her beautiful eyes. "She just totally stood up to me. Hmm, maybe I'll marry that girl one day."

Readers, at that point in my life I was full of shit. I could have just as easily of said I was going to have sex with that girl in the back of my car one day.

Chapter 2

Sex . . . . Crying . . . . and a Hot Shower

My line of work allows me to see a whole lot of messed up things. One day I will be treating somebody for a blade wound and the next George and I will be carrying out a balding man on a gurney, while his dog is literally stuck to his zipper. I would go into more detail, but I really don't want to piss off the dog lovers out there. Poor Ibaka, I would never let that happen to you!

To help get these terrible, fucked up things out of my head I used to depend on wine and a steady dose of easy women. Luckily for me, this business is full of drinkers and I get to meet a lot of women willing to show me how grateful they are that I saved their life or their skin from scarring.

About a year ago, I was called out to a middle class neighborhood where I had the sublime pleasure of meeting Kate. She's blond, 6 ft. tall and has legs that should be illegal in at least 20 states. Oh yeah, she's also married to some overweight banker and I saved her kid's life. Blah, blah, and blah!

I know what you're thinking. I shouldn't have been sleeping with somebody's wife. I should respect the sanctity of marriage. You do have every right to hate me, but I told myself I was performing a valuable service for Kate. Her husband hadn't been able to see his own dick in a decade, she has two kids that run around the house like morons on a Cinnamon Toast Crunch high, and she was just really in need of somebody who cares. She needed somebody who listens to her. She needed somebody who can respect how sexy her body really was despite the grubby kids. I was that somebody for her. The fact that we fucked like rabbits in and around her house is merely a fringe benefit. I really am a giver!

On one particular night, my sexy distraction was free because her husband was out of town on some business trip. Kate always ripped on her husband, because he had to buy two seats when he flew. I once asked why she stayed with the fat fuck, I mean her husband, and that resulted in a month of no distractions at her place. I'm a quick learner, so I didn't broach that subject again!

It was 10 P.M., so her two kids were sound asleep. She would always leave the back door unlocked, so I could let myself in and have a seat in her kitchen. Now, never tell a MILF that you are hungry, because they always feel the need to feed you. Kate is no different. Every time I was over at her place there were always a sandwich and a bowl of soup waiting for me. She's fond of saying I need my strength after a long day of saving lives. Yet, I was never actually given the time to eat before the main event began.

That night was no different. Within moments of sitting down at the kitchen table, Kate appeared in a fluffy green robe decorated with turtles.

"Follow me," she said, gesturing for me to follow her into the laundry room.

"A robe," I said, with a disappointed look on my face.

"Shut up!" She replied, smiling like she had just robbed a bank and got away with it. "I have a surprise for you."

I do very much like surprises, so I followed her into the laundry room and closed the door behind me. Kate turned on the dryer and proceeded to disrobe, showcasing a delectable and sexy black and red corset underneath.

"Do you approve?" she asked, self assured at what my answer would be.

Readers, I know watching a sex scene on a dryer looks 12 kinds of hot in the movies, but in real life the logistics just suck. It's all about the height and weight factor of both people involved. Basically, you find yourself doing the math in your head, which seriously challenges the blood in your body from going down South. This can be a problem, especially for you older men out there.

Anyways, I'm not a big fan of chit chatting during play time, so I showed my positive reinforcement by going over to her, bending her over and . . . .

"Mommy!" Her child screamed, from the other side of the house. "Where are you, Mommy?"

"Hold on," Kate said, before putting her robe back on and going out to check on her kid.

Now, I'm a big fan of MILFs and what they stand for, but the whole kid thing can really throw you right back into reality. It was time for a cigarette and I had the perfect place. Kate's chubby hubby had recently built a pretty sweet shed in the back yard. She told me this is the only locked place for them to fool around. I know thinking about Kate fucking her hubby is just wrong. I really don't want to think about how that whole mess worked.

After about 20 minutes, Kate joined me out in the shed. I had been distracting Kate from the horror of having sex with her husband for a while, so I knew she needed a moment to get out of mommy mode and back into "I want your cock inside of me right now!" So, I had a cigarette waiting for her and as usual, it did the trick nicely.

"Are you ready to try this again?" She asked, her sexy smile had returned to her face and she began to take her robe back off.

"Come over here," I exclaimed, while staring at her corset like I was about to unwrap a present on Christmas day.

Kate is excellent and very talented when it comes to pleasing a man. Still, there are rules you have to play by when performing with a married woman. Luckily, you have me to share the juicy details. First, never ever leave marks. This really becomes important when the husband is ugly or out of shape and has no self-esteem. These husbands have a tendency to check their wives' bodies

13

like a hawk for bruises, hickeys and other love making reminders. Second, do not say anything that will remind the woman that they are cheating on their husband. I know this sounds odd, but a quick reminder of reality can halt steamy play time faster then a teenage boy who is about to lose his virginity to a girl way out of his league. Last and possibly most important, make sure you have your entire basis covered when it comes to birth control. If you get her pregnant, you might as well start practicing your bitch slapping for that lovely appearance you'll be making on 'Jerry Springer.'

In addition to the major rules, most married women bring their own rules to the table and Kate was no different. She felt that traditional vaginal sex should be saved for her husband. So, she's only interested in having anal sex. I guess this helps Kate convince herself she's not really cheating. For me, I had the added convenience of knowing she couldn't get pregnant (See rule 3).

So, for the next couple of hours that night, Kate and I took turns exploring each others bodies. She felt so good and it was a lovely, sexy, dirty way to end the evening. Oh, I almost forgot something really, really important. If you're a dude and want the debauchery to be an on going thing, make sure she gets off at least three times. Trust me, anything less and you're replaceable. Anything more and she might fall in love with you and then you have a whole new set of problems.

Upon finishing the dirty deed, I stuck around for a few minutes to catch my breath and pondered what was next on my schedule. Kate is a hugger after sex and that is a major no, no when it comes to fucking another dude's woman. Men, if you find yourself in this situation, make sure you have excuses you can put in play at anytime. Stay away from the early work day excuse. For me, my job was the built in excuse. If you were to ask Kate, she would tell you I get called out to a scene just about every night. Generally, or luckily in her opinion, I don't get work calls until 10 or 15 minutes after we get done having sex. Kate is so sexy and so very gullible when it comes to my excuses. I love it! If you don't have a nifty excuse like me, keep it simple. I will demonstrate for you rookies out there.

"I really have to take a piss," I said, cutely performing the pee pee dance in front of Kate.

"We can go back inside the house if you want," Kate said quietly, trying not to fall asleep in her shed from my earlier performance of awesomeness.

"That's okay sexy, you stay here and rest," I replied.

Upon uttering those words, I got up, found my clothes and made my escape for the evening. I really did have to pee.

I returned home that evening after a quick stop off at Wing Run for some food, beer and a potty break. As usual, my Boxer dog, Ibaka, was at the door waiting for me. I found him without a tag or a chip on the side of the road. He was dirty, but in great health. Ever since then, he's been a great pal and an excellent listener. Plus, he almost never bitches back; unless I forget to feed him. Ibaka can be a complete diva when he hasn't been fed.

I'm stalling right now because I don't know how to broach this subject with my readers, without losing some of my coolness factor. I'm in my earlier 30s, pretty damn sexy and have a sweet pad in a nice part of town. My life is pretty fucking good, or at least it should be, right? Well, my life's ups and downs have been as dramatic as Lady Gaga's costume changes.

I guess the best place to start is by telling you that I'm a big fucking hypocrite. On the outside I'm a complete Ashton Kutcher look alike. Okay, would it be easier to believe if I said I'm a young Mandy Patinkin look alike?

"You killed my father, prepare to die," I said, pretending to duel with my confused puppy.

Anyways, I'm getting off point. On the outside, I can pretty much fool anybody into believing I'm a self-confident guy. I had years of practice and money to make sure my teeth and self-esteem would end up in top notch condition by adulthood. But then May 1st happened and that all went away with just one phone call.

The next day was May 1st. To honor this momentous occasion every year, my brain overrides my body and I'm a hot mess. Actually, I would be more precise if I called myself a wet mess. You see it was that day, three year ago, my phone started blowing up while I was in the shower. My girlfriend at the time liked to call and text me a lot, so I would always bring my phone into the bathroom with me just to avoid the where were you questions if I didn't happen to answer the phone. I'm such an asshole. To be fair, I wasn't as big of a jerk back then. I needed more seasoning and life gave me that in spades on that particular Friday. There is nothing I wouldn't give to go back to that day. I could have done so many things differently. Look at me. I'm a mess from just thinking about what happened. I'm crying like Kate's child after a nightmare. Maybe because it's my own personal nightmare that I can never ever wake up from. I could have been a better boyfriend. I should have been there. I should have said so much more. I could have saved . . . .fuck me, I don't ever deserve to wake up from this nightmare.

Again, I'm getting off point and I apologize. So, I was in the shower and my cell started to blow up. I stopped humming to whatever Foo Fighters song was playing in the background, opened the shower curtain, and grabbed my phone. Why was I fucking listening to the Foo Fighters at that moment? I never fucking listen to music while I'm in the shower. That day was different. That fucking day was going to be special. My favorite band was getting me pumped up and I had already picked out the wardrobe I was going to wear that evening. I was going to look good. I had been planning this for a really long time and everything was going to be perfect.

I have no idea if I have any readers out there. If you are reading this, just know I have given my heart to two women and Julie was my first. In both situations, my heart has been smashed. It's apparently very dangerous to love me.

Anyways, when I answered the phone the first time all I heard was screaming. I figured it was one of my jerk friends playing a prank on me because they knew this was going to be a big, huge day. So, I hung up and started belting out more words to a Foo Fighters song. For the life of me, I truly can't remember which song. At that time, I knew every word to every fucking song in their catalog and I can't remember the fucking name to one Goddamn song!

My phone quickly rang again. This time I could make out what the person was saying on the other end. It was Julie's dad. I had just spoken with the man two days earlier. But this conversation was very different. Mr. Johnson sounded so sad. I could tell he was choosing his words carefully. I wanted to interrupt him and tell him I was kind of indisposed at the moment, but when he started to weep on the phone my mind started to race. He said there had been an accident. Mr. Johnson said I needed to get over to their house as quickly as possible. He said. The fucker said. Excuse me for a second. Okay. He said Julie was gone.

I suppose I should have been better at taking the news. After all, I had just become an EMS worker a year earlier and the grief training and multiple exams were still fresh in my mind at that point. Yeah, I'm not sure anybody can truly be trained to handle their own grief.

I only remember tidbits about what happened after I received the call. I remember dropping the phone on the floor. My legs felt really fucking heavy, so I sat down in my tub. Was it "Times Like These?" No, that doesn't sound right. I can't remember that fucking song. Fuck, fuck, fuck, fuck! Jesus, why can't I remember that song? I do remember turning the shower faucet to extremely hot, but I felt nothing. I just sat there in the shower thinking about everything and nothing all at the same time. I was sure this wasn't really happening. Julie wasn't really dead. She couldn't be. There is no way somebody so perfect . . . . What was I suppose to do without her? Who the fuck am I without her in my life? She was my muse. She gave me the ability to breath and at the same time could take my breath away with just one touch.

"Ian, where are you?" A male voice said, it was muffled by the sound of the shower.

The voice kept calling out to me, but I couldn't answer. It was like I didn't know how. Every time I would have a thought, it was erased by a steady flow of sobbing and the realization that if I allowed myself to calm down, reality would sink in and Julie would be dead. Finally, my friend Robert peeked his head into the bathroom. I remember wanting to ask him for help. I'm pretty sure I did a couple of times in my head.

"Ian, I'm so, so sorry," he said.

He handed me a towel, found a chair, and just had a seat. I will never forget the melancholy look on his face until the day that I die. Perhaps, this is that day.

"Mr. Johnson just called me," he said, trying to hold back tears himself. "He wants me to give you a ride over to the house, but take all of the time you need."

The rest of that day was in slow motion. Robert helped me get ready and then drove me over to the house. My parents were already there. So many people were there. My friends were there. Julie's family, friends and neighbors were there. Even the priest . . . the man

who was going to . . . . I mean he was supposed to . . . .
fuck! This hurts so damn bad. I can't stop crying.

I suppose it should have been comforting having
everybody there. Each person was very kind and told
me if I need anything, anything at all, to just ask. It took
me a while to not hate people for telling me that. All I
wanted to do was scream at these people that no, they
couldn't do anything. The only person in my life who
could was fucking gone. The woman who was going to
be mine for . . . . Well, that just wasn't going to fucking
happen now. I loved Julie more than I loved myself.
Some asshole made sure that our love wasn't going to
last and then drove away.

If you're reading this, know that I'd like to think
time heals all wounds. That the pain I feel every single
fucking time a Foo Fighters song comes on the radio,
will one day go away. But why the hell should the pain
go away? It was my fault! I should have been there. I
could have done something. Now, it has happened all
over again. I mean, I'm jumping ahead in the story.

"Come here Ibaka," I said, looking for some furry
comfort. "It's time to go to sleep."

Chapter 3

Here Comes the Bride

It was the third anniversary of Julie's death. Every year I think that if I can make it through today, maybe I will be just fine. Perhaps, this will be the year that it starts to hurt a little bit less. Maybe, I'll get through the day and know there was a purpose or a greater plan for my life. Who am I kidding? Why should I just delay the inevitable?

There was one thing I had going for me this year and it's Robert's wedding. He proposed to his fiancée January a while back and she wanted a May wedding. Robert asked me if they could have the ceremony on the first, as a way to take away a little of the pain this day holds for me. Plus, this was the only Saturday in May that their dream church isn't booked. Being the top quality best man that I am, I humbly said yes and added that this would be considered my wedding present to them. After all, I do so hate buying gifts.

The day was going to be fucking busy and all I really want to do is curl up in the corner of my bedroom, drink a bottle of wine, and pretend I was somebody else.

Every year, I start the morning by jogging around the cemetery where Julie is buried. Her parents are always there first thing in the morning and I just can't face them. They leave a message for me to join them and each year I never return their call. Instead, I choose to jog around the grounds until they leave. Last year, they stayed all morning. Like a dumb ass, I chose to just keep jogging until they left. I suppose I could have taken a break or just went home, but it just never entered my mind. I guess in some perverse way, I like seeing them. I just can't face them; not after what I did to them a few weeks after Julie passed.

The Johnsons finally departed and I could make my approach. I jogged toward her grave sight and as I got closer my heart began to beat in overdrive. Tears started to flood down my face. This wasn't supposed to be us. She was going to be a professor. I had my EMS job and we were going to be that happy successful couple that you see in the movies. Julie wanted two kids, a house outside the city and a swinging chair on the porch she and I could call our own.

I dropped to my knees in front of her grave. Her mom is a clean freak, so Julie always has the neatest looking plot in the cemetery. Each week, Mrs. Johnson would bring fresh carnations and stick them all-around her tombstone. Julie loved carnations. She would always say roses were pretty, but carnations were built to last longer. Just like us. She was right about a lot of things, but in this case I guess we were roses and she was wrong.

Her parents asked if I wanted to help choose what was written on her tombstone. It was just too hard to say yes. I'm no where near worthy to be making decisions like that. There were many nights I would wake up with thoughts about what should have been written. Here lies the greatest thing that ever happened to me or here lies a girl that touched the heart of every person, place, and thing she'd ever met. Her parents decided to go with something simple, honorable and very sweet.

Here lies Julie Johnson. A loving daughter, friend, and fiancée. Her love and spirit will never be forgotten.

My mother was the first person to tell me what the Johnsons had decided to put on her tombstone. She said they considered me family no matter what and that's why they wanted to include the word fiancée. If you were to ask me today what I think about that, I would probably smile and say I was very thankful for their generosity. I didn't have that exact reaction back then. I immediately hung up with my mom and called Mr. Johnson. All I was feeling at the time was pure rage.

Mr. Johnson invited me over to their place and I raced right there.

It was two weeks after Julie had died and I hadn't been back to their house since that horrible night. I sped into the drive-way and didn't even turn off the car. I'm sort of surprised I even remembered to put the car into park. All I knew was hate at that moment and I was going to erupt like Mount Fucking Doom.

Mrs. Johnson was at the door to welcome me, but I walked right past her. I was angry, but I wasn't going to take it out on her. I had a certain father in my targets and nothing was going to stop me.

"Hey there, Ian," Mr. Johnson said, looking somewhat distraught.

"What the hell gives you the right," I said, struggling to get each individual word out of my mouth. "I never proposed. I never fucking got the chance!"

"Please," Mr. Johnson said.

I was in no mood to hear about what he was thinking or his reasoning. I just wanted to give him a piece of my mind. I wanted him to see just how dead inside I was and I didn't need him advertising to the world that Julie died before we could start our life together.

"How dare you write something like that?" I said, looking for something to throw or punch. "Every fucking time I go to visit her, it will be a reminder about how I will never see her walk down the . . . . or say I . . . . or be able to kiss the . . . ."

At that point I was hyper-ventilating and crying at the same time. I couldn't get full sentences out of my head; much less my mouth.

"Ian," Mr. Johnson said, putting his hand on my shoulder. "She loved you more than anything or anyone else and you two didn't need a ring to prove that one day you would end up married."

He was right. The man is a damn doctor, so it wasn't exactly shocking, but that didn't stop me from taking his hand off my shoulder and punching him straight in the nose. He's a small, balding man, so he went down to the ground like a sack of potatoes. Mrs. Johnson heard the commotion and walked into the room to see what was happening.

"Fred, oh my gosh," Mrs. Johnson said, racing over to check on her husband. "What the heck is going on?"

"It's fine, my dear," Mr. Johnson said. "It's just a misunderstanding."

Okay readers that might have been the worst thing I've ever done in my life. Mr. Johnson is a generous, loving man who has never been anything but wonderful to me. Even with the pain I was feeling at that point in time, he didn't deserve to be punched by me. Plus, I wasn't done yet.

"No," I said, trying to catch my breath. "The misunderstanding is you two thinking I want to have any fucking thing to do with you!"

Trying not to fall to my knees and beg them for forgiveness, I stormed out of the house. I knew even then that I wasn't the least bit mad at them for anything. Her death was on my watch. How do you look into their eyes and beg and plead for forgiveness?

Luckily, my still running car in the drive-way hadn't been stolen and I sped away down the road. That was the last time I ever stepped foot in that house or spoke to the Johnsons in person. In addition to the messages they leave each year inviting me to join them at the cemetery, I sometimes will see their number pop up on my voice mail without any messages. I think it's their way of checking up on me.

After I left their place I raced directly to the cemetery. I needed to speak to her. When I arrived to her grave sight and saw the word fiancée for myself, I dropped to one knee. I pulled out a box from my jacket. You see, I couldn't force myself to get rid of her engagement ring. It was all I had left of our future together and I kept it on my person at all times.

"I knew you were perfect for me from the second time I ever talked with you," I said, opening up the box. "I don't deserve you, but you will make me the happiest man on this Earth if you would marry me."

Yes, I was proposing to a tombstone. I just felt cheated. Everything was planned. I was going to take her camping. She loved to go camping and we had made love for the first time in front of a camp fire. It had taken us forever to build that fire. Still, it was one of those perfect nights. I was going to build a camp fire and after making love to her, I was going to pull out the ring and propose. Instead, I was given bad news by her father, while standing in the shower.

Anyways, kneeling at her grave sight I chose to believe that she would say yes. I put the ring back in its box and dug a small hole with my hands. I placed the box in the hole and told her she would always have my heart. Every time I return to her grave, I'm always tempted to dig and see if the box is still there. I never do because I hope our love will one day be able to rest in peace.

"I love you Julie," I said.

I had a wedding to go get ready for and a groom to pick up. It was time for me to get my shit back together.

I honestly had no idea how I was going to react at this wedding. Could my insecurities about this day really be put aside for sake of my friend?

So, I headed back to my place to get ready. Ibaka was there to great me. He even did me the courtesy of tearing up some Kleenex and leaving it for me at the door. His way of saying welcome home person who gives me food and forgot to feed me. I cleaned up the mess and put on the tux. Half way through struggling with my tie, my legs gave way from under me. Is this whole thing just too much for me after all? No, you're fine, just stop being an asshole. Get your stubborn, sniffling ass up! I needed to be at Robert's house in like, 20 minutes.

Despite my pre wedding hesitations, I did reach his house with two whole minutes to spare. When I arrived, Robert was freaking out in his bedroom.

"Thank God you're here, bro," Robert said, pacing like a mad man. "The catering people just called and said we have an ant issue!"

"Are they attacking?" I said, not really sure what else to say.

"Ass!" Robert promptly replied. "The caterers said ants torpedoed some of our candy almonds and ruined our wedding party favors on the tables. January is going to be pissed!

"So what are these caterers doing to fix the problem?" I asked.

"I don't know," he said, his body was literally shaking.

"Okay, give me their number and I'll take care of this," I said, going into a surprising take control mode. "Then go finish getting ready. You are marrying a very special girl today!"

Now, one big part of being a best man or a best friend in general is knowing when to tell little white lies. That was definitely one of those times. January is an interesting cat. She comes from money and her attitude suggests she is better than any of Robert's friends. January is also not terribly attractive. She is blonde and does having large breasts. Unfortunately for her, the rest of her body has caught up to her breasts since college and she shows no signs of putting the biscuits down. Hell, she hated me before I even met her, or so Robert told me on one drunken evening. Supposedly, I had wronged one of her friends. I still don't remember how and she has been determined to hate me ever since. If I wanted to be an ass, I could have done nothing about the reception ant madness and blame it on somebody else, but I wasn't that guy on that day. For whatever reason, Robert saw something in the bitch and she makes him happy. So, I called the caterers and with a little sweet talking and $250 dollars, the problem was going to be fixed and sanity would be restored to the universe.

I walked into Robert's room and he was sitting on his bed. I suppose that could have been me sitting there, scared to death about marrying Julie. Nah, I don't think I would have been nervous. Things with her were always so simple. She knew how to navigate my emotions and was always there to keep me calm. She would put her face directly in front of mine and just stare and smile at me. She wouldn't let me move my face until I smiled back at her. Even when I was trying to be obstinate to her stare, I could never hold out for very long. It really was hard being mad for too long around that woman.

"Look at the handsome groom," I said, trying to calm the nervous best friend down. "I fixed the reception problem and they told me everybody will now get twice as many almonds. There will be an avalanche of almonds if you will."

"Oh, I didn't know you're a funny man," he said, pulling at his ridiculously tight bow tie. "Thanks. Dude, do you think I'm ready for this?"

It was time to pull out the best friend white lies play book, but which one shall I use?

"Of course!" I said, with a reassuring smile on my face. "January is a great girl, who loves you very, very much. Plus, she's not bad on the eyes either."

It was his day, so why not pull out the she's pretty white lie. That poor, poor bastard just doesn't know what was in store for him. Although, I did have a tendency to judge her a little harshly at times, but I will never admit that out loud.

"There is no need to have cold feet," I said, now grabbing his jacket and handing it to him. "In just a few minutes you'll be standing beside the girl of your dreams and saying I do. This is going to be a good day."

Readers, I hadn't thought of Julie in like, an hour at that point. I had been staying busy and on point with the wedding. Then Robert had to go and ruin my momentum.

"So, how are you doing?" Robert said, while trying to broach the subject I'm so trying not to think about. "Did you go to the cemetery this morning?"

"Yeah, I was there," I said. "Dude, seriously, this day is about you."

"Well hey, let me know if you need to talk at all," he said.

"Thanks, but let's go get you married."

It was off to the park. Luckily, the Oklahoma May weather had stayed pretty mild. We arrived and were immediately escorted to a tent behind the wedding site. Robert's brother, Todd, joined us in the tent moments later.

"How are you two old losers doing," Todd said, with a little girly cackle. "When is this fucking wedding starting? And where are all the fine bitches?"

Now, it's important for you to understand that Robert and Todd couldn't possibly be any more different. Robert is 29 years old and is 10 years the elder to his Goth brother. Robert was Mr. High school football. Todd is more likely to be putting on eye liner and writing bad poetry, then attempting to play any kind of sport. Oh, and Robert told me he once overheard his mom call Todd a mistake. I'm telling you what, if you give anybody in Robert's family the least bit of alcohol, they really will tell you anything you want to know.

"So, does it bug you to have to wear a tie that is adorned with a primary color?" Robert said, mocking his little snot of a brother. "What, no make-up?"

Robert's mother required her eldest son to have his brother as a groomsman. Something about family bonding or some bull shit like that.

"Mom's not letting me wear any you freak," Todd said.

Robert and Todd really don't like each other. These two bicker at each worse then an old married couple. With that in mind and 30 minutes before the ceremony, I figured it was a good time to make my escape and go smoke a cigarette.

The park really was beautiful and there were ample places for me to hide, relax, and take a smoke break. It was starting to get late, so the children's playground was empty; a perfect refuge. I climbed into one of the big toy slides and blazed up a camel. I was doing real good thinking about absolutely nothing for once, when somebody's voice rudely interrupted me.

"Can I get a drag of that?" a female voice said, very quietly.

I remember turning around hoping it would be a sexy single woman.

"Oh, it's you," the girl said, as my face came into view.

"Do I know you?" I said, realizing right away it was Liz, the girl who had thrown me out of her dad's suicide.

"Stop even trying to pretend you don't remember me," she said, impatiently. "So, can I have a drag or not?"

I handed her my cigarette. She looked so fucking beautiful despite donning one of January's ugly as sin purple dresses. She had her hair down and it just swayed in the wind, exposing her sexy neck.

"So, how do you know January"? I said, trying to fill the silence.

"She's my cousin and I'm one of her bridesmaids," Liz said "How about you?"

"I'm actually the best man," I said, showing her the ring I was supposed to keep safe. "So, what are the odds, huh?"

Liz took another drag of the cigarette and sat next to me. She smelled so good. It was the perfect combination of berries, melons, and hotness.

"So, are you here with some poor female victim you met out at a crime scene?" She asked, with a snicker, like she was proud of the zinger.

"No, I'm here alone," I quickly replied. "I'm fresh out of victims."

"Well, I suppose you can always find some poor unsuspecting girl, here," she said, again seemingly enjoying spraying zingers my way.

Readers, this may seem silly, but I enjoyed the witty back-and-forth banter. I didn't know Liz at all. She might have been crazy; after all she did throw me out of her house while in the process of flirting with me. Still, something just felt right about being this close to her, and I don't mean I wanted to jump her bones. Well, I didn't want to jump her bones just yet.

"Look, I'm sorry about how I came off at your house," I said, showing remorse, or at least doing my best impersonation. "I'm not really that guy."

Liz put her arm around me for a split second and gave me a wicked Cheshire smile. Her face is so expressive and I could feel the coolness of her hands as they brushed by my face.

"That's too bad," Liz said, while reapplying her lipstick. "I think men who know what they want can be very, very sexy."

Again, she flashed me an evil little smile. Damn, she looked so fucking good, but before I could reply to her advances, we were rudely interrupted.

"Liz, is that you on the slide?" A male voice said, in a very angry tone. "The wedding is starting in like 10 minutes."

"I'm sorry honey, I just lost track of the time," she replied.

"So, when you say honey, is he your brother?" I asked, hoping for a response not ending with boyfriend or fiancée.

Liz reached back down and planted a kiss on my cheek. She grabbed her purse and started to walk away.

"I'm here with my fiancée," she said, turning her head towards me to comment. "Thanks for the smoke."

What just happened? I was left dumbfounded on a children's slide, holding a cigarette butt in one hand, and hiding my large . . . .with my other hand. Had I found my match at my best friend's wedding. Either way, I needed to get back to Robert before the wedding started.

The outdoor ceremony started without a hitch. The men got into position by the pastor and the wedding party made their way down the aisle. The whole ceremony was only going to last about 15 minutes, but that depended on how long January decided to make her vows. That girl likes to hear herself speak. Still, as Liz slowly walked down the aisle, I found myself wishing this was a Catholic ceremony and we would have to be here for at least an hour. She looked so fucking stunning. I'd like to tell you the bride looked equally as good, but I shall not tell lies in the presence of a minister.

I had one duty during the ceremony and that was to hand Robert the ring. If I had been paying attention to what was going on, it was a job I should have accomplished with very little effort, but when it came time to hand my friend the ring, his pesky brother had to punch me on my arm. What the hell was wrong with me? I've only crushed on one woman in my entire life; Eva Green notwithstanding. I just couldn't stop looking at Liz, who was standing five feet to my left. Did I have a thing for this beautiful, intoxicating, lovely, and graceful woman? I suppose it didn't matter. She does have a fiancée, but on the other hand that had never stopped me before.

Chapter 4

A Tricky Little Dance

The reception was in a huge tent on the other side of the park. The wedding party finished up taking pictures and we all made our way to the festivities. Once inside, I found the open bar and decided the best way to get Liz out of my head was to drink and drink heavily.

It was a very nice reception with over 150 people shoveling food into their mouths and getting shit faced. I managed to find a quiet table in the corner and sat my ass down with a brandy in one hand and two shots of tequila in the other. It was time to get drunk and scope out any pretty single women that may want to have some sloppy, depraved wedding sex. Unfortunately, the pickings were slim and I had already been with most of the cute, single girls under the tent. I'm not a big fan of re-runs.

Dinner service had come to an end, all of the boring speeches had been made, the cake was cut, and now it was time for the DJ to get people out onto the dance floor. Perhaps I may have missed a single girl I hadn't slept with on my first go around, so getting all the ladies dancing will give me a second chance to survey the room. Nope, I was right the first time. I needed a smoke, but before I could leave the tent, somebody grabbed my hand.

"Where do you think you're going?" a female said. It was Liz, I was absolutely sure of it.

I turned around and sure enough Liz was standing there, holding my hand. I could feel goose bumps building up all over my arms, but at the same time her touch game me a sense of calm.

"I'm headed out for a smoke," I said, starring directly into her deep blue eyes. "Do you want to come with?'

"No, I want you to dance with me," she said, with a vivacious smile causing her face to glow.

I nodded my head yes and we made our way over to the dance floor. We were still holding hands. It was a slow dance, so she gently crossed her arms over my head and we began to move as one. It had been a while since I had slow danced, but everything seemed so easy with Liz. Even her lack of height wasn't an obstacle as I lifted her onto my feet, so I could look into her eyes. I hadn't noticed it earlier, but she had little clusters of freckles on her face. Boy, I was crushing hard!

"So, where is your fiancé?" I asked, breaking one of my rules by bringing up the other man. "Won't he mind you dancing with me?

"He had to leave for work," she replied, positioning her head onto my shoulder. "Besides, it's not like I'm kissing your neck or touching your ass."

This fiancé is a better man than I am. If I was engaged to a self-assured girl like this, I would not leave her alone at a wedding looking this damn yummy.

As the song started to wind down, I could feel her lips get ever so closer to my neck. My body started to spark with anticipation of what might come next. Was I going to get that kiss after all?

"Forgive me if this is too forward," I said, ever so quietly. "You look simply amazing, tonight."

Before Liz could answer or choose to ignore me, the song wound down. I started to let go when Liz kissed me once on my neck. It was quick, but soft, and it made every hair on my body from my toes up to my head stand up in attention. Since Julie, I have been with many, many women. In fact, I've probably been with too many women. Still, not one of them has made my blood boil or my heart start racing like Julie had every single day. Liz kissed me just once. Some might even just call it a peck at best and only to my neck. Yet, that feeling of joy, hope, and a sense of future came rushing back to my brain. Perhaps it was the combination of booze and the happy feeling I always hear about being associated with weddings? Or perhaps I still had a beating heart left in my body after all.

The next song was the 'Chicken Dance,' so we both promptly hustled off the dance floor. I needed to go outside, smoke a cigarette, and collect my thoughts. She had other plans in mind for the remainder of our evening.

"Well, thanks for the dance," I said, starting to part ways. "I'm going to go say goodbye to the groom,

Colleen Michaels

smoke a cigarette, and then probably go home. It has been a long day, but it ended on a happy note."

"Hold on a minute, dear," she said, grabbing my arm. "Why don't you go say goodbye to Robert and then maybe we can go back to your place and hang out?"

I so, so wanted her to come back to my place. Were we going to fuck? Was she just trying to be friendly? How clean did I leave my place? More importantly, how clean had Ibaka left my place?

"That sounds like fun," I said, trying to hide all of my anxiety that was undoubtedly filtering into my words. "Why don't you just meet me out in the parking lot in like 10 minutes? You can follow me to my house."

"I will see you in 10 minutes," she said.

I set out to find Robert and possibly have a heart attack. Everything seemed to be rushing through my brain at he same time. Still, the image of our slow dance seemed to be ninja kicking all other thoughts from existence. She was so fucking beautiful. This girl was making me mental.

"Dude, are you doing okay?" Robert said, walking up to me with concern on his face. "Is this whole wedding thing starting to get to you?"

"Um . . . . I have a girl stuck in my brain," I said, studying each word as it popped from my mouth. "It's not Julie."

"Why are you looking so doom and gloomy for?" He retorted. "You're always thinking about fucking a new girl. Why should today be any differ . . . . ?"

Robert had stopped in mid sentence thinking I was distraught over today being Julie's. . .you know. I suppose I shouldn't have been thinking about Liz.

"That Liz girl is waiting for me," I said, not really knowing how to explain this to him. "She's going to follow me back to my place."

"January's cousin, Liz?" He said. "Isn't she like married or engaged or something?"

"It's not like that," I replied, deciding to keep my feeling toward her a secret.

Robert had a confused look on his face. Still, he slipped into best friend mode and didn't press me for any answers.

"Well, thanks for coming man," he said, giving me a bro hug. "Just be careful. I think Liz's significant other is a fireman and they know how to throw down."

So, I had made my goodbyes and started to make my way toward the parking lot. Liz was already waiting for me when I arrived. She was puffing on a cigarette and playing with her cellphone.

"There you are, handsome," she said, with a smile that could light up the night sky. "You're not one of those guys that takes forever to go anywhere, are you?"

Chapter 5

Making Popcorn . . . . Not Love

We reached my place and my mind was still racing in anticipation. I opened the door and there was Ibaka to set up the first test. Did she like dogs? Is she allergic? Will she even acknowledge the existence of my furry little friend? Before I could get all of the questions out of my head, Liz was on her knees playing with Ibaka. He was a good bullshit detector and she had him eating out of her palms.

"So, he seems to like you," I said.

"Oh, I love dogs," she replied, with a tone of affection. "You're such a good puppy. Yes you are."

Okay, she passed test number one with flying colors. She had to have some flaws. No girl is this hot and this together.

"Can I get you something to drink?" I asked.

"Didn't you say something about being a wine drinker?" She said, with an evil grin on her face and biting her bottom lip.

"Did I?" I said, playing coy and trying to show off my cute charisma. "I think I can handle that."

I went to my wine rack and grabbed a bottle. Liz decided to make herself at home, dropping her purse on the floor and placing her watch on my table. She seemed comfortable enough as she began searching my living room for things that she enjoyed.

"Where did you get that painting?" She exhaled out, pointing at a picture of Elizabeth and Mr. Darcy from "Pride and Prejudice."

"I think I got that on my trip to England several years back," I retorted, doing my best to show I'm sophisticated. "I thought it would look nice in my living room."

Okay, readers, I confess to being a bit of a romantic. I know my actions so far have suggested otherwise, but fuck you. There is nothing wrong with a grown man itching for a little romance in his life. Of course, I wasn't going to tell her that.

"Are you done yet?" Liz said, pointing at my cork opening process.

"Are you in a hurry?" I quickly replied back.

"Well then," she exclaimed with authority, while walking over to her rather large purse sitting on my floor. "I'm going to go change into something a little more comfortable."

Without asking for directions, Liz proceeded into my bathroom and shut the door. As for me, I finished pouring the wine and started to wig out a little bit in my head. Should I put on some mood music? Is she going to walk out of the bathroom wearing lingerie or better yet, nothing at all? I'm going to put on some music. Yes, that seems like the best plan. Wait, maybe she is more of a TV person? So, I turned on my TV and let my body merge down into my couch. Before I could get too comfortable, my bathroom door swung open with authority.

"So, what do you think?" She said, pointing at her white fluffy robe and Snoopy slippers.

"You got anything on underneath that mopey robe?" I asked.

Liz quickly opened her robe and flashed me, displaying a t-shirt that looked at least the same age as her. Despite the meager look, Liz pulled it off.

"What did you think I was going to be wearing underneath?" Liz questioned, once again biting the bottom of her lip.

"I was expecting nothing," I replied. "Do you want to drink this wine or not?"

Despite having at least five different places to sit, Liz chose the cushion right next to me. She positioned herself Indian style on the couch, grabbed one of the glasses, and took a sip. Seriously, it was though we were old friends and she'd done this a million times before. Yes, she was making me nervous because I have never met a girl like this before. She seemed so damn self assured in her t-shirt and slippers. She'd put her hair in pigtails, so I took the opportunity to scan for any kind of flaws on her face, neck, and ears. This girl is absolutely amazing.

"So, how come you don't have a girlfriend?" She asked, breaking the silence. "Or are you not the significant other type?"

As Liz finished her sentence, she ever so slightly raised her pajama bottoms to itch her leg. Although her legs were pale and somewhat bruised, they were in shape and amazingly lovely to look at in rotating bursts. It would be so wonderful to run my hands up her legs. Fuck! Why does this girl have me crushing to damn hard?

"I did have a long term relationship once upon a time," I said, rather quietly for some reason, "but that's a story for another day."

Liz took another sip of her wine. She laid back on my couch and rested her feet on my lap. She just seemed so comfortable with being near me. Honestly, I felt like roles were being changed around. Usually I'm the one in charge, and in that case I was just taking a back seat to her.

"Do you have any popcorn?" she asked, showing off her smile that seemed to cripple me the more I saw it on her pretty face.

"Yes I do," I replied.

I sprung up from the couch like I was on a mission. Get a grip, Ian. This isn't the first beautiful woman you've ever had in your place. She won't be the last hot girl, either.

"So, do you want salt?" I said, thinking about anything and everything to ask her that didn't include will you please let me kiss you.

Liz got up from the couch and walked seductively in my direction. She picked up a single kernel of popcorn and gently placed it into her mouth.

"No, it's perfect," Liz said, while licking her lips. "So, tell me about this mysterious ex of yours. Was she better looking than me?"

I started to fidget with the popcorn. If I tell her about Julie, there is no chance of getting laid tonight. If I lie, she can always find out the truth from her cousin. So, I chose plan C.

"So, you're engaged," I said, hoping she would let me get away with changing the subject. "How long have you two been together?

Liz gave me an evil grin before grabbing the popcorn bowl out of my hands. She quietly made her way back over to the couch. Was she judging me? Did she think I was making Julie up? She sees me as a player. I could fix that with one story about Julie. Well you see Liz, Julie broke me so fucking bad that I have to take depression meds every day just so I don't wonder if six feet isn't so far down.

"I will answer your questions about my fiancée, but afterward you have to tell me what your ex did to you," she said, almost beaming, due to her brilliant plot. "Do we have a deal?"

Liz held her hand out and I shook it begrudgingly. Her hand was freezing cold, despite the warm weather outside. Still, I liked having her hand in mine. It was a sensation I hadn't felt in quite some time. Don't get me wrong, I've held females hands since Julie. Karen the MILF is quite the snuggle bug and hand holder, but somehow, something just felt right embracing Liz.

44

"So, we've been dating for two years," she said. "We met at my restaurant. Eight months later we were engaged."

"You own a restaurant?" I pondered.

"I wish," she said, half punching my shoulder. "I'm the head chef at La Belle downtown."

Okay, this continues to become more and more unfair by the moment. For the readers at home, let's recap Liz's accomplishments. First, she's absolutely beautiful. Second, she seems to have things together and is getting married. Finally, she's an accomplished chef. The only thing missing is a tap on her body that flows chocolate milk. This girl was perfect and taken.

"So, when is the big day?" I asked, keeping the questions coming.

"We still haven't set a date yet," she said, rolling back into the cushion. "That's a whole other headache."

Her foot started to move ever so softly against my leg. Was she flirting with me? Is play time at Disney World Liz about to commence? Wow, that was really bad, but then she stopped, stood up and started to walk around like she was nervous.

"So, how about you?" She said, with her evil grin once again showing. "We'll start with something simple. What was her name?

"Julie." I said.

"How long were you two together?" She responded.

"Six years," I said, purposely being short with my answers.

"Were you two ever engaged?" He responded, again.

I remember sweat starting to build on my brow. I didn't like the questions. It was ruining the moment. I didn't want to think about Julie.

"It's my turn to ask the question," I said, with a sense of entitlement. "You answered two questions and I answered two questions."

Liz started to laugh uncontrollably at my insinuation that I had any say in the matter, but she played the game quite well. She took a sip from her wine glass.

"This is yummy" she said, looking so damn cute. "Is this an '88?"

"That's a good palate you have there," I replied.

"So, shoot," She said.

"Excuse me?" I replied.

"Ask your next question, silly man," she said, laughing.

"Okay, does he treat you like you deserve to be treated?" I asked.

Liz seamed to be put off by the question. Maybe I had gone a little too far with the question? Or perhaps she has seen right through the question and knows I'm crushing on her? Still, Liz quickly composed herself.

"He can be a very loving man," she said, her lips were attempting a smile. "We have our issues like any other couple. You have one more question!"

"What do you look for in a man you date?"

Fuck it. I'm an inquisitive kind of guy. Why not ask the question? Besides, she's over at my place right now. Maybe I do have a shot! I could totally be some girl's type.

Liz seemed to like this question. She began to move around the room, with a big smile on her face. It was as though she was taking an exam and was sure she knew the answer.

"Well. . . .they need to have a sense of humor," she said, pointing at a picture on my desk with Ibaka and I dressed up as Batman and Robin. "They need to be self-sufficient, caring, and it doesn't hurt if they are monsters in the sack."

Wow, Liz and I could actually be great together. I fit that mold and I had a host of girls who can be references for my abilities in the bedroom. Well, maybe not a huge list, but I have been known to be a man-whore by a few people that know me.

"So, I guess your fiancé fits that bill?" I asked.

Liz walked back over to me. She bent over and put her mouth right next to my ear.

"Buzz!" she yelled, with a big heaping grin covering her face. "It's my turn now, my dear."

She was so close to me and smelled so darn good. All I wanted to do was reach over and kiss her. Why not go for it, Ian? The worse thing she could do is slap you. No, play this cool and answer her questions.

"After being together for six years, were you two ever engaged?" She asked.

"We were going to be," I answered, once again going back into short answer mode.

Liz's face was once again inches away from mine. I could feel every breath she took. I could count every single cute freckle on her cheeks.

Then she asked the question I wasn't ready to answer; "How come you two aren't married?"

I stood up, grabbed my wine glass, and took my time with my answer. I really wanted to kiss Liz. After all, I am a warm blooded male and this is what we do. Should I tell Liz the truth and ruin any shot of that happening.

"It's a long, long story," I said, hoping she would leave it at that.

"I'm tipsy and in my slippers," Liz quickly retorted. "You have the floor, good sir."

"Honestly, if I tell you, it might ruin any chance of us" . . . . I paused.

"Of us . . . . What?" she responded.

Now there are two questions floating around the room that I don't want to answer. Fuck! I didn't know what to do.

"It would ruin any chance I have of kissing you tonight," I belted out.

Oh damn! Ian, you are a fool. Good looking, but you're a damn fool for saying that. Now, she's so going to leave and this whole evening will have been for nothing.

Instead, Liz stood up and made her way over to me. She had a sexy, almost devious grin on her face. Liz grabbed my shirt with both of her hands and held on to me real tight.

"What exactly did you think was going to happen tonight, stud?" She asked, in a similar tone to a sex phone operator. "Were you expecting just a kiss or did you think you might round third base and head for a home run?"

"Honestly, I wasn't expecting anything to happen," I said, trying to think about old people, soft ball players, and back acne in my head.

I wasn't completely lying to her. I really wasn't expecting anything to happen. Still, I'm not ashamed to say I was certainly hoping for some kind of wedding night magic.

Liz let go of me and went and grabbed her bag and jacket. She appeared to be getting ready to leave. Damn it! I went too far and now I've offended her. With the exception of her goofy slippers, she was now prepared to leave and she walked back over to me. Liz dropped her bag at my feet, leaned in real close, put her lips millimeters away from my ear, and then grabbed my ass firmly with both hands.

"If I had been planning to kiss or fuck you, believe me, you would have zero doubts in that handsome brain of yours," she said, making every last part of my body tingle.

Liz picked her bag back up, opened the door, and turned back around. She still had that same devious grin on her face.

"You still owe me an answer to that question," she said. "But I'm a patient girl."

Liz leaned over and kissed me on my cheek and then she was gone. We hadn't even exchanged phone numbers. Damn! I think I might like this girl.

Chapter 6

Flipping the Perception Switch

It had been a week since Liz walked out of my place. I wonder if she was thinking about me? I wonder if I will ever see her again? I couldn't get her out of my mind, my thoughts and my dreams. How did I let her leave without getting her number? Shit!

"Dude, you are being very quiet this morning," George said, while getting into the driver's seat of our EMS mobile. "Did you forget to take your meds again?"

George started up the truck and we headed out on duty for the evening. Should I broach the subject with George? He would probably just call me a dork and laugh. I hate married people. They're always so smug and think they know everything about relationships. Still, this girl has been on my mind all week. I needed to tell somebody.

"So, I met a girl at the wedding," I said, gently wading into the conversation.

"Good for you," he replied, with a goofy grin on his face. "So, what's the problem?"

"I didn't get her number," I said, sounding sort of pathetic.

No sooner then I got those words out of my mouth, a call came to us from dispatch. It was a domestic dispute. George flipped the siren on and it was time to get down to work.

"Did she know anybody at the wedding who you know as well?" George asked.

He had raised an important point. Perhaps January would tell me where Liz lives. They're cousins after all, but, January also hated me.

"Yeah, she's January's cousin," I said, half hoping George would talk me out of asking her.

"Oh, that bitch!" George shouted, shivering as he thought about her. "Is she anything like January? I really, really hope not."

Liz was nothing like January. She leaves you wanting more and more. This is the opposite of her cousin, who leaves you wanting to find a hammer and some duct tape.

"How was she in the sack?" George blurted out, before I could finish my train of thought.

"No, we didn't sleep together," I replied, momentarily holding onto the thought of her climbing into my bed. "It was more than that. I think I might dig this girl."

We had arrived at our destination and were waiting outside until the cops gave us the all clear. George turned off the truck and looked at me very intensely. I knew a lecture was coming and I really didn't want to hear what he had to say after all.

"Ian, you just met the girl and you think you like her already?" George started to shake his head. "It sounds to me like you're reaching. I bet, if you had gotten her digits, you would probably never call her."

I would like to mention how sad it is when grown men use the word digits, but the police gave us the all clear. We grabbed our gear and proceeded over to the house. As we walked by one of the cop cars, I could see an asshole screaming in the back of a squad car. I hate domestic calls. There is always too much yelling and drama.

"Here we go," George said, slowly opening up the door. "Don't think you've gotten out of our conversation, by the way. I have more to say to you later about this girl."

We walked inside and an adult female was lying on the kitchen floor crying. Her face was swollen and her arms appeared to be heavily bruised. I leaned over to take a closer look.

"You poor thing," I said, trying to comfort her. "I'm here to help."

I started to assess her wounds when the patient carefully put her hand on my arm. Something about the feel of her touch seemed familiar.

"Ian?" She said, so quietly that I didn't make it out at first. "Is that really you?"

"Yes, it's me," I said, and then I realized who it was I was treating.

"It hurts so much," she said, trying to inch herself closer to me.

"Stay still, sweetie," I said, while trying to keep her calm. "I promise . . . . you're safe now. I won't let anybody else hurt you."

I needed to stand up and get my mind straight. As I attempted to move, the patient grabbed on to me tightly.

"Please don't go," she whispered, tears continuing to flow down her face.

"I will be right back," I said, slowly removing her arm from my shoulder. "I just need to speak with my partner real fast. I will be just a few feet away."

I motioned for George to come over and speak with me. He quickly complied with my attempt at sign language.

"What's going on?" George asked, with a puzzled look on his face. "Why do you look like you've seen a ghost?'

"That's her," I whispered, trying to hold in my emotions that were starting to turn into rage.

"That's who?" He quickly replied, still sporting an inquisitive expression.

"That's Liz, the girl I was telling you about in the truck," I said, as thoughts of grabbing a baseball bat and beating the piss out of her fiancé continued to prance around in my head. "Look what he fucking did to her."

George's puzzled look changed quickly to worry. Few people outside of my immediate family knew any details about what had happened to Julie and the number it had done on me. George is one of those people. I could tell his big heart was slumping down into his chest.

"Do you want me to handle this?" George asked, almost looking like he was about to hug me, but didn't know how to embrace another man. "You can handle crowd control."

"No, I told her that I would stay with her," I quickly retorted. "I'm a professional. I can handle myself."

I was mostly telling the truth when I told George I could handle myself. Liz was in need of my help and after Julie, I told myself I would never let another woman in my life get harmed again. Okay, so I've only met this girl a handful of times. Still, the alpha protector in me was on red alert that evening. I was definitely ready to throw down.

Liz was shaking as I sat down to treat her wounds. At first, I could tell she wasn't comfortable with another man touching her. I would try to dress or bandage one of her wounds and she would tremble in terror. Still, after a few minutes I could tell she was starting to feel just a little safe again. Her crying had started to slow down, which left her face glistening from the tears.

"We're going to need to take you to the hospital," I said, as I finished up everything I could do in the field.

"Will you go with me?" Liz asked, while grabbing onto me in pure terror. "I really don't want to be alone."

"No problem," I said, trying to give her a reassuring smile. "Is there anybody else you want me to contact? Any family or friends you want to meet you at the hospital?

"No," she said, tears began to trickle down her cheeks again. "I don't want anybody else to see me like this."

So, George and I helped her onto a stretcher and started to wheel her out to the ambulance. The asshole was still sitting in a squad car as we made our way outside. I could feel Liz's hand tremble as it gripped tightly onto mine.

"Don't look at him," I whispered, into her ear. "I won't let him harm you anymore."

We loaded her into the ambulance, but I didn't want to leave just yet. My mind was clear of congestion and now all I was feeling was rage. How the hell could he beat on this beautiful girl? Well, now I'm going to beat on him a little. I think George could tell what I was feeling because he made sure to stand in the direct path between me and the asshole I was going throttle.

"Just get into the truck," George said, starring intensely at the door. "It will do her no good for you to get arrested. She has already seen enough violence for one day."

It might not do her any good, but I know I sure as hell would feel a lot better. Still, I listened and got into the back of the ambulance with Liz. After a few minutes of driving, I gave her some pain medication and she drifted off to sleep.

"Sweet dreams beautiful girl," I whispered, trying to get my mind off the sense of rage I felt. "Things will be better when you wake up."

Liz was out for the next eight hours. I sat alone in her hospital room waiting for her to open her big blue eyes. Readers, seeing her like that just crushed my heart. When Liz was at my place, she was this gleaming star of self-confidence. I don't think she stopped smiling all night long. Now, she was in a hospital bed. The bruises on her face masked the beauty underneath. She looked like a completely different person. Yet, I had this overwhelming feeling that I needed to protect her.

Just as I was about to go ask a nurse for coffee, Liz slowly opened up her eyes. It took a second for her to figure out her surroundings.

"You stayed," she said, trying to show me her smile.

"I told you I would," I softly replied, walking over to her bedside. "How are you feeling?"

"Like I just lost a boxing match," Liz said, trying to muster a laugh in the process. "You should see the other guy."

"Can I get you anything?" I asked.

"I just want you to stay here and keep me company," Liz replied, reaching out for my hand.

My heart started to melt as I stood next to her, and I tried to separate the bruises from the absolute beauty I knew was underneath. I had been searching for her ever since our night together. Now I had found her and she needed me.

"So, you must be my guardian angel," she said, while starring into my eyes.

"Why do you say that?" I asked.

"Because you always seem to be around when I need you," she replied, with a grin. "Even if you do try and hit on my sister during the process."

She squeezed my hand and goose bumps raced all over my body. Looking past the fucked up situation, this just felt right. Liz needed me here and I wanted to be here with her.

"Well, your sister isn't here now," I said, with a grin on my face. "Is she?"

Liz brought my hand up to her mouth. She was still favoring her left arm. She gently kissed my hand. Then she looked up at me with those sapphire colored eyes of hers.

"Thank you," Liz said, with a real sense of sadness and thankfulness on her face.

"We've shared popcorn together," I said, trying to put a smile back on her still pretty face. "That means we're pretty much best friends now. Anytime you need me, I'll be there."

Liz smiled, but then let go of my hand. A strong sense of despair seemed to grip her body. She no longer looked me in the face.

"I bet I look awful," she said, while looking around for a mirror. "I can only imagine what you must think about me. I bet you're glad I didn't give you my phone number now, huh?"

She tried to get up, which exposed several bruises up and down her arm. The swelling had gone down in her face, but the asshole had really done a number on her pretty . . . .

"Was that him sitting out in the police car?" I asked, half hoping it wasn't.

Liz slowly looked down. I could tell she felt ashamed. I wanted to comfort her, but was I just making things worse by bringing it up? My job training had completely abandoned me and now I was just hoping she would say anything.

"He's really . . . . we've been together . . . ." Liz said, trying and failing to defend her asshole.

She slumped back down into her bed. She pulled her sheets up close and hid the rest of her face with her hands. At that point I was certain all I was doing was making things worse.

"He's only done this one other time," she said, quietly through her hands. "He promised he had taken classes for his anger."

I sat down beside her on the bed. These things are made for models. No way two grown adults can fit comfortably on these beds, much less comfort each other. I gently put my hand on her back. She seemed to welcome the contact.

"You shouldn't go back there," I said, almost sounding like I was commanding her. "Do you have a place to stay?"

"I think so," she responded, faintly.

Readers, this is when things went from bad to what in the living fuck is happening!? The asshole made his way into the room. He had two bouquets of red and pink roses in his hand. The asshole was even dressed up. Too bad he was about to get blood all over his jacket.

"Wow!" I said, standing at attention. "What the hell are you doing here? Nurse, I need you to go get security right away!"

"Wait!" The asshole shouted, pulling back with both hands up and looking at Liz. "Sweetie, please hear me out! Please, just give me five seconds."

I started to walk toward him. Both of my hands were in fist formation and I was about to go Johnny Cage on this mother fucker. I could totally take him, whether he was a fireman or not. I was sure of it. But then Liz stopped me.

"Ian, no," she said, once again trying to sit back up. "Let him talk."

"But . . . ." I said, not really knowing what else to say.

Security entered the room. I told them this was the guy who had beaten the fuck out of the patient. I'm pretty sure I was a little more eloquent than that, but it doesn't really matter.

"He's all right to stay," Liz said. "I'm not in any danger."

The security guards glanced over at me.

"This is her call," the security guard said.

"He did that to you Liz," I said, my voice and blood pressure where rising as one. "He should not be allowed around you."

"Don't think you know me," she said, getting ticked off. "We have been together a long time and he loves me. Don't you dare judge me."

"I think you'd better leave," the asshole said. "You are upsetting my fiancée."

59

Colleen Michaels

I looked over at Liz. For just a moment she flashed me a look. The type of look that shouts I'm sorry . . . . but there is nothing I can do. Liz was defeated.

"Ian, please just go," she said, quietly and without hope.

[Readers, I may have substituted Asshole in for something else, but humor heals wounds my friends. When that doesn't work, try tequila. For the remainder of my tale I will refer to him by his proper name of Asshole.]

I begrudgingly made my way out of the room. It was truly an out of body experience. All I wanted to do was kick Asshole out the window and yes, save the damsel in distress, but my princess told me to get the hell out.

Chapter 7

Drinking . . . . a Good Friend . . . . and Morning Surprises

Robert's return from his honeymoon was a welcomed one. Unfortunately for my liver, it was about a week too late. Since Liz kicked me out of her hospital room, all I had done was go to work, come home, and get shitty drunk. Even Ibaka had started to stay away from me as my depression had become a real downer.

I haven't heard from Liz since that day. There was once this week that I got a prank call from an unknown name, but I didn't hear anything on the other line. I suppose it could have been her, but most likely it was just a wrong number.

There were a couple of times that week that I expected Asshole might try to make a stink with me. After all, he really didn't like me being at Liz's side at the hospital. During my drunken moments, I even rehearsed how I would react if he made an appearance ay my place. Depending how drunk I was at the moment, I was either going to cuss him out or beat him

Colleen Michaels

down with a straw, a baseball bat, and this cord from my video game system.

Asshole never made that trip over to my house. Neither did anybody else. I was starting to believe everything was going back to the way it was before I'd met Liz. Still, that time period was when I started to write this tale. There is nothing wrong with being a single, attractive male who happens to have a cushy job. I really should have been happy or at the very least content with myself, but here is this tale telling me otherwise. Readers, I needed help at that point. I could no longer tell if my meds were working or not. All I knew was being sober wasn't an option.

I made my way to the bottle and began to play a drinking game with myself. For every truly fucked up thing that had happened to me, I had to do a shot. Believe you me, after a short time I was really, really shit faced.

Just as I had gotten done with a wonderful rendition of 'Where in the World is my Dog Ibaka,' there was a knock at my door. Who would dare knock on my door at 3 A.M.? Shit! Has Asshole finally made his way over to my house to confront me? Oh, I'm ready for you. I tried my best to stand up and get tough, but my legs and brain weren't actively on the same page. It was pointless. Somebody kept knocking on my door, but I couldn't get over there.

"Ibaka, answer the door for me buddy," I said, half motioning toward my dog.

He decided staying put was a better idea. It didn't matter anyways because I heard the door unlocking.

62

"Are you alive in here?" Robert said, sounding a little bit concerned. "Ian, are you home."

I dragged myself up into a standing position. Thank God, somebody human to speak with about all of this shit.

"What are you doing here?" I asked, and I'm almost completely sure that's what I said.

Robert made his way into the kitchen and found me drunk and my place a mess. His first reaction was to get the bottle away from me. Admittedly, I didn't make it easy for him.

"I thought you weren't getting back until tonight?' I said.

"We made it back early and I thought I would swing by and check on my best man," he said. "Did I miss the high school party that trashed this place? It stinks in here, dude."

"Well then, this calls for a toast," I said, raising the bottle in the air.

"I think you've had enough, buddy," Robert said, being sympathetic and annoyed at the same time.

"No, I'm just toasting you, man!" I shouted. "This is a time for celebrating!"

I grabbed the bottle back from Robert and after one last swig, my legs gave out, and I fell on my ass. Robert quickly took the bottle out of my hand. I was drunk, sitting in filth, and now my ass was hurting.

"So, I called George and he told me what happened," Robert said.

"George, George, Georgey," I said, completely stalling while waiting for something smart to pop into my mind. "George has a way of sticking his nose into other people's business. Besides, what does he know?"

I tried to crawl my way over to the couch. Readers, I'm well aware how pathetic it is to be in my 30s and have to move my drunken self one lunge at a time. I managed to rest my head onto the couch, but gave up after that.

"George told me you have a thing for . . . ." he said.

"I knew he would open his big, fat mouth," I said, interrupting Robert. "Yes, I found what or who I thought was somebody special. Robert, I was very, very wrong."

Robert made his way over to me. He grabbed my arm and helped me get my carcass up on my comfy sofa. Robert then sat down on a nearby chair and continued.

"He told me about what happened to Liz," he said, choosing each word like he was under oath. "George said you were a fucking hero to her that day."

"Some hero I turned out to be," I said, perturbed at myself. "She chose a man who beats the hell out of her over me and all I did was walk away."

Robert got back up from his seat, grabbed a blanket and put it over me. He had gone into best friend mode and wasn't really paying attention to what I was saying.

"You tried to help out a girl who was in trouble," Robert said, with real empathy in his eyes. "You went way out of your way to make sure Liz was safe. "You can't control how she's going to choose to react."

He was making a good point, but I was drunk and tired, so over reacting was on the menu. Plus, when I'm going through my crazy period, it's not a good idea to mess with me without extended training. Between Julie and now Liz, Robert was board certified to deal with me.

"Why is it that every girl I care about ends up getting hurt in the end?" I said, for no real reason other then to be dramatic.

"Have you been taking your meds?" Robert replied, while thinking he had immediately diagnosed my problem.

"I've been drinking," I said, sticking my hand up in the air and giving the Hawaii gesture for hang loose, I think. "That's all the medicine I need to take."

Robert gestured for me to sit up. I complied with his request, putting one arm around his shoulders. From there, Robert dragged me into my room and laid me down on my bed.

"First, you need to get some sleep, dude," Robert said. "When you wake up, you need to take your Goddamn pills. I'll leave them for you by some aspirin and a glass of water."

Robert left the room for a moment, but quickly returned. I had heard his phone ring while he was gone, but I didn't hear what he was saying. It was probably January. I was sure she was telling him that I was a lost cause and to go the fuck home.

"Robert . . . . I think I'm broken," I said.

He grabbed a chair from my desk and sat down beside me. The man never looks upset, even when he has to stay up all night taking care of my drunken ass.

"Dude, you're not broken," he said, sounding reassuring. "Close your eyes and get some sleep. I promise things will be better when you wake up in the morning."

I awoke the next morning and my head was pounding. I'm guessing Robert had opened up my drapes and the sun was shinning through the window. It was like being in my own hangover hell.

Stumbling to my feet, I heard noise in the kitchen. Before I could investigate what Robert was probably burning, I noticed two aspirin, my crazy pill and a glass of water sitting on my coffee table. Sitting next to my hangover remedies was a note telling me to take my meds and then head to the kitchen. Boy, Robert really has girly damn handwriting. Maybe, he called his wife and she's here cooking breakfast? Fuck, I really don't want to deal with January at that point.

I entered my kitchen and there were two suitcases at the entrance. I know my place is nice, but there is no way that couple is moving in here. Best friend or not, his wife is a...

"Good morning, sleepy pants," a female voice said, a female voice that sounded a lot like Liz. "Did you see what I left for you on the coffee table?"

I immediately stopped in my tracks. First, I rubbed my eyes and prayed I was wearing my nice boxers. Score, I wasn't looking half bad for being hung over, in need of a shower, and only wearing my boxers.

"Um, I didn't expect . . . . I mean what are you . . . ." I said. "Good morning."

While I had been sleeping, Liz was in my kitchen cooking enough breakfast for a legion of Roman soldiers. She had the kitchen set up and there were serving dishes on my table containing pancakes, eggs, bacon, and sausage. Readers, I didn't even know I had owned serving dishes until I saw them on my table.

"I didn't know what you like," she said, flashing her Cheshire smile. "So, I made a little bit of everything."

I picked up a pitcher and there was honest to God freshly squeezed orange juice inside. Obviously, both of us were stalling at that point. My wits had come back to me, but I wasn't ready to broach the subject as to why she was in my kitchen. Liz was finishing up dishes and singing Lady Gaga songs like she had been doing this kind of thing in my kitchen for months.

"This is perfect," I said, sitting down at the table. "Why don't you join me? There is enough food here to feed the Packers."

Liz continued to dry off dishes. I wonder if she realized I owned a dishwasher?

"I'm not really hungry," she said, working hard to keep that grin on her face.

"I don't want to eat by myself," I shot back, getting up and pulling out a chair for her to sit down.

"I don't like to eat when I'm nervous," she said, shaking her head at my attempt to get her to sit down. "It's a really nice morning. It might be a good day to take a walk."

As she was doing busy work, I could tell she was wearing a lot of make-up and was being careful how she faced me. She kept referring to the nice weather, yet she was wearing a long sleeved turtle neck.

"I think we should go take a walk," I said. "Let me go put some clothes on. It's not good for me to scare the neighbors."

"What about your food?" She replied.

"It will be there when we get back," I said, heading out of the kitchen and toward my room. "We'll both be hungry after exercising!'

I threw on some shorts and a T-shirt, before joining her back in the kitchen. Liz was still sporting a smile on her face, but I could tell she was also studying every expression on my face. It was like she was in a courtroom and getting ready to be judged by me.

"Let's go for a walk," I said, while opening the door and offering my hand.

Liz seemed a little apprehensive at first, but then flashed me a confident smile and walked right past me and out the door. She was obviously hard-headed, but that wasn't always a good thing for Liz.

"You better be able to keep up," she said, already half way down my drive-way.

I jogged my way over to her. I could now see all of her face. The swelling and bruising had gone way down. The superficial beauty Asshole had taken from her was returning in spades.

"So, should I start?" She asked, covering her face in apparent embarrassment. "Where do I begin?"

"You don't owe me an explanation," I said, but still hoping she would provide one anyways. "I'm not here to judge you."

A Manic Kind of Love

Liz reached over and hit me on my arm. She laughed once, exposing her great beauty to the world and then started looking around in front of her.

"I've owed you an explanation since the hospital craziness," Liz said, her facial expression had turned back to a serious tone. "I owe you a lot."

We had reached a nearby park and Liz motioned for me to follow her over to the slides. Tulsa had spent a lot of money cleaning up parks for families to enjoy. Everything was brand new, right down to the dirt under our feet.

"This seems like an appropriate place for a talk," she said.

Liz got comfortable and I sat down on a nearby swing. She seemed to be going around in circles in her mind as to how she wanted to start the discussion. Several times she put her head up to speak, only to put it back down again and say nothing.

"It's really pretty out here," I said, trying to break the silence.

"So, I finally left him," she said, a couple of tears started to roll down her cheek.

"Did he do something else?" I asked, starting to tense up.

"No, but we had an argument and I could see he wanted to," she said, as tears began to slide down her face like rain. "He left the house mad and said he didn't care if I was still there when he returned. So, I packed a couple of bags and . . . ."

"You showed up at my door?" I said, interrupting her in mid sentence.

I hopped up from the swing and made my way over to her. Liz looked up at me and all I could see was hurt coming from her eyes. She was scared and alone. So, I sat down beside her and put my arm ever so gently around her back. At first, she seemed worried about me touching her, but after a few moments I felt her relax into my arms. It always took her a little time, but she seemed to always feel safe with me. Readers, putting the shitty circumstances aside, it felt like heaven on earth having her in my arms.

"Robert was leaving your place and saw me sitting at your door," she said, once again putting her hands over her face. "I didn't know where else to go. He told me to come inside . . . . that you wouldn't mind."

Liz began to openly cry. I was sitting there holding her. There was so much I wanted to tell her. Liz didn't have to feel unsafe around me. I would always protect her from fuckers like Asshole.

"I'm glad you felt safe coming to my place," I said, whispering into her ear. "You will always, always be welcome."

As I finished my sentence, she took her hands off of her face. I don't care that she still had bumps and bruises, Liz was one of the most beautiful people I'd ever seen. Her face was soaked in tears, but the gentle smile on her face gave me reason for hope.

"So, what happened to Robert last night?" I asked, hoping he wasn't still at the house and I had completely ignored him.

"He left shortly after bringing me into your house," she said. "He said to get some sleep and that everything would be better in the morning."

"He said the same thing to me before I passed out last night," I said, with a goofy grin on my face.

"Was he right?" she asked, while standing up and grabbing my hand.

"He was absolutely right," I said.

At this point we were inches apart from each other. Readers, I really, really wanted to kiss her, but I didn't. The timing didn't seem right and I wanted her to know it wasn't about anything physical for me.

"The last one back to the house has to clean the dump," Liz said, with a gleaming smile. "Your place really smells."

Then she took off jogging toward my house. Fucking Robert . . . . I really do hate it that he's always right. In this case he was right twice.

Chapter 8

Our First Date

Readers, three days had gone by since Liz started bunking with me. Each night was a little weirder than the next.

On night number one I thought it would be best to set up some ground rules.

"Rule number one . . . . Asshole is not allowed over here ever!" I said, feeling like I was laying down the law. "That includes phone calls while in this house. Ibaka doesn't need that stress in his life."

Liz didn't seem to have any objections. She just curled up on the couch and continued to look into my eyes. Fuck, what's rule number two?

"Rule number two . . . . we have to work out a bathroom schedule, so there isn't any . . . . you know," I said, sounding very much like a child.

Again, Liz didn't seem to have any issues with the rule. In fact, she got up from the couch and joined me on my cushy large chair. Seriously, she just got up and walked over to me. So, here we are in my living room and there is a girl I'm completely crushing on curled up in my arms. It was absolutely perfect. Still, being the moron I am, I didn't stop to appreciate the moment.

"Rule number three . . . . what exactly is going on with us?" I said, both turned on and confused by Liz. "Are we just friends? Are you flirting with me and this is you showing that?"

It was answer time. At least I thought that was going to be the case right up until the point I noticed Liz was sleeping on my lap. She didn't hear the last question. I guess she wasn't flirting with me after all. This is why it's not easy having depression issues and a beautiful girl who may or may not like you. There is just way too much second guessing that goes on in my brain.

The second night started out innocent enough. Liz said she was a big fan of board games. She especially liked the game Life, because . . . .

"If you make bad choices, you can always start over," she said, while biting her bottom lip. "You can't do that in the real world."

Luckily for me, my father had bought me a new board game every time he went on a business trip while I was growing up, so my closet was full of games. We spent half the night playing Life, Monopoly, and Hungry Hippos. Perhaps the night was answering my questions from yesterday. Maybe, she wanted us to just be friends. Then things started to take a turn for the weird when Liz suggested our next game.

"Oh, you have Twister," she said, now licking both of her lips in a very, very sexy way. "We totally have to play this next!"

So, I put my left hand on green and for the next 30 minutes, participated in a very sexy tango with Liz. I swore at the time we weren't actually having dry sex during some of our leg on red and left ear on blue situations. Still, looking back at it I can't be so sure. Liz's back started to tense up, so she suggested one last game.

"It's for all of the marbles," she said, with a wicked, wicked grin on her face. "It's a good ice breaker. Are you up for it?"

"What did you have in mind?"

"Get me a pack of cards," she said, while having a seat at the table. "The game is Texas Hold'em. If you lose a hand, you take off an article of clothing."

Her wicked grin remained on her face. Let's see, how many articles of clothing am I wearing? How many articles of clothing is she wearing?

"I'm in," I said, confident I would be seeing naked Liz real soon.

Yeah . . . . that didn't work out too well for me. You see six hands into the game and I was wearing six less articles of clothing. I was down to my boxers and a smile. I had three-of-a-kind, but once again she was able to beat me. Liz put a full house down on the table and then stood up.

"All right," she said, with a big smile. "I believe I've hit pay dirt. Now strip off those boxers and do it slowly."

I hesitated for a second, but I didn't have anything to hide. So, I began to pull down my boxers when Liz stopped me.

"I just wanted to see if you'd do it," Liz said. "Interesting! Well, I'm going to bed."

On the third night, Robert and January invited us over to their place. My head had been spinning from the previous couple of nights, so some time with my friend sounded nice and a lot less stressful. I was so very wrong!

"How are you two getting along?" January asked. "Has he been acting like his dorky self?"

Readers, there are a lot of ways Liz probably could have answered that question. She could have talked about how she had me wrapped around her little finger, or she could have joked about my snoring or adverse reactions to anybody peeing with the door open, but she didn't.

"He has been amazing," Liz said, while looking straight into my eyes and smiling. "I don't know what I would have done had it not been for Ian."

"You could have stayed with us," January said, being a huge bitch!

January's numerous barbs aside, the night was a lot of fun. Liz spoke about me as if I were somebody important. She was sweet, caring, and sounded as though she had feelings for me. I think Robert caught on to what I was thinking because . . . .

"Hey Ian, help me with the trash," Robert said, motioning me toward the kitchen. "I have a bad back."

Ian and I went outside and each lit up cigarettes. I could tell he had something on his mind. He always knew me way too well.

"So, what's the deal with you two?" Robert asked. "She seems to really dig you. Have you two been good boys and girls?

"We've been saints," I responded. "Honestly, I have no idea what to do next! Robert, I like this girl."

Robert took a puff of his cigarette and let it out slowly. He seemed to be contemplating his next step. It was fun to watch him deep in thought. I swear you can actually see his mind churning.

"You two need to go out somewhere," he said. "Ask her out on a proper date. Give her a romantic evening she won't forget."

Robert likes to go a little bit overboard with his speeches, but he was right. Again! I needed to ask Liz out. We needed to do something special to see if what we had was something more than just pals.

Liz and I left the dinner party about an hour later. It was nice outside, so we decided to take a walk. Neither of us was tired and it gave me a window. With the stars out in spades that evening, it gave me a romantic window.

"So, can I ask you something?" I said.

"You just did," Liz responded, with a smile. "Sure, of course."

"I think we should go out tomorrow night," I said, counting Mississippi's in my head until she answered.

"We went out tonight," Liz answered, at four Mississippi.

"I mean . . . ." I replied, getting cut off before I could finish.

Liz put her arm out, which stopped our stroll. She took off her slippers and stood on top of my feet. She had a look of anticipation on her beautiful face.

"Are you asking me on a date?" Liz whispered, in an amazingly sexy tone.

"Sure . . . . I mean yes," I said. "I very much want to take you out."

Then it happened. Every light in the area was extinguished at the same time. I no longer could hear sounds or see anything or anybody but her. It was just for a brief moment, but Liz leaned into me and we kissed. There are so many times where the actual moment doesn't come close to the expectations. This wasn't one of those times. It was subtle, restrained and so fucking sexy. Her lips just sent shivers up and down my body.

"I thought we should get that out of the way," Liz said, once again licking her lips ever so slightly.

She then got off my feet and put her slippers back on before grabbing my hand.

"I think we should just keep on walking," she said. "I could get used to holding your hand."

So we did and it was amazing to hold her hand and walk in silence. Every once in a while Liz would put her head on my shoulder and my heart would pump a thousand times harder. We reached our house and the night was over. She got ready for bed and then retired into her room. I also went into my room, but I had a date to plan and a night to reflect upon. It had been a very good evening.

Colleen Michaels

Readers, as I said before it has been a weird past couple of nights. If I had been a gambler, I would have foreseen date night going in the direction of strange as well. Instead, I was focused only on Liz.

The night started out splendidly. I told her to grab the door when she heard a knock around 7 p.m. I wanted to pick her up, just like any other first date. Liz did wait a second before opening the door, but when she did . . . .

"So, what do you think?" She asked, while spinning around slowly, seductively.

She was wearing a pink evening gown that flowed down her body. Her hair was hanging down her neck. She had on a light lipstick, but very little else in the way of makeup. In other words, she looked perfect.

"You look wonderful, my dear," I said, motioning at her to look behind me.

Now, my job has its share of flaws, but you also make some good contacts. In this case, a friend of mine at a limo company owed me a favor. You see, a rich client of his almost died while "experimenting" with coke a couple of years back. It wasn't pretty, but let's just say I helped him out discreetly and ever since I get two free nights of limo rides per year for the rest of my life. I'm going to be honest, it's pretty fucking awesome.

"Wow, very classy," Liz said, while wrapping her arm inside mine. "Where are we going first?"

The first event of the evening was reservations at this four star sushi restaurant downtown. I'm not the world's biggest sushi fan, but I can tolerate it and I know it's her . . . .

"How did you know sushi was my favorite?" She asked, looking very excited about my first choice. "I never told you that, but very impressive."

Readers, I'd like to think I am that impressive . . . . but I'm not. You see, during our first meeting at Robert's wedding, Liz went on and on about how this was the only other restaurant she would openly call impressive in this city other then her own. Still, since that time she had apparently forgotten all about that conversation.

"I think Robert told me or something," I said, coming up with a believable excuse. "I'm glad you like it. You really do look very good I might add."

Okay, judge me if you want for lying to her, but I really didn't want to begin the evening by reminding her she forgets shit. I'm so getting off track here and I apologize.

So we dined at a nice restaurant and it was everything I had been expecting. There were no nerves on my part. I felt comfortable having her sit across from me. She was the best looking person in the room and best of all she liked being there with me.

"That was amazing," Liz said, finishing the last bite of her sushi roll before sitting back in her chair. "What's next on the agenda?"

"Once a year my partner throws this huge street party," I said.

"Sounds great, but aren't we both a little over dressed?" She answered back.

"I was prepared for your question," I said. "I asked January to pick out something appropriate for the party. I hope you don't mind."

I pulled out a garment bag that had blue jeans, a button down shirt and a cowboy hat. I do love me a fine looking country girl.

"There's also some boots in this bag," I said. "His parties are kind of a homage to Johnny Cash."

Liz didn't say a word. She had a devilish little grin on her face. She grabbed the bag and motioned with her hand for me to look the other way. For the next few minutes we both got dressed into our country gear. I swear from time to time I could feel her turn her head around and take a peak. Perhaps, she was making sure I wasn't peaking?

"Okay, you can turn around whenever you're ready," she said.

I turned around and I instantly had a new found appreciation for January. You see, Liz looked . . . . I couldn't believe this girl was with me. Her legs were sexy in the jeans and boots. Best of all, her cowboy hat caused a glare on her sexy freckles. She was a true country beauty and for that night she was mine.

We arrived at the party and the festivities had already started. The Johnny Cash tribute band had already played their first rendition of "A Boy Named Sue." It was a beautiful Tulsa night. There was just a little bit of wind. The smell of BBQ was coming from every drive-way up and down the block. My partner was in front of his grill. You could tell he had already had three too many.

"Ian, there he is!" George said. "Get over here buddy! Who's that with you?"

"George, this is Liz," I said, hoping he would remember the conversation we had earlier in the day about me bringing her and him not embarrassing me. "She's my beautiful date for the evening."

"Oh, of course," George said, while smiling. "Ian has not stopped talking about you at work."

"Really, you haven't huh?" Liz asked me, while tugging at my shirt.

"George, remind me to have a conversation with you about tact tomorrow," I said, while looking a little embarrassed.

"No, don't be mad at George," Liz said, while grabbing my hand and squeezing it reassuringly. "I think it's sweet."

Before I could change the subject, the band came back from their break and began to play again. As though they were sheep, three quarters of the party merged around the band and began to dance.

"Shall we?" Liz said, while looking at the dance floor.

The next several hours consisted of a consistent pattern where we would dance, drink, and then dance some more. I hadn't had that much exercise since gym class. Still, I'm not ashamed to say that I held my own on the dance floor and Liz seemed to be having a great time.

"I can't believe how amazing you've been," she whispered, as we danced to a slow song. "You barely knew me, yet you wanted to protect me."

Colleen Michaels

"I don't know what you want me to say?" I whispered back. "You were in trouble. There was just no way I was going to let him hurt you anymore."

"Come down here," Liz said, pulling me to come down to her level.

Liz kissed me. It was long. It was intimate and it should go down into the hall of fame for kisses. I swear the band's music was now a soundtrack for us locking lips. Readers, I really, really like this . . . .

"I think I like you, Ian" Liz said, sliding her head onto my shoulder. "I don't know quite what to think about that, but I definitely think I like you."

It was late and time to go home. George was passed out in bed, so we found the limo. Now, this is where the big limo sex scene generally happens in stories. Think Kevin Costner and Sean Young in "No Way Out." In this story, something better happened or at least more romantic. Liz laid her head down in my lap and I just sat there watching her sleep. It had been a wonderful night and a successful first date.

We reached the house and the driver opened up our door. Liz was still sleeping so I picked her up and started to carry her toward the house. This is when shit got weird.

"Oh, this is just fucking perfect," a male voice said, one that sounded like Asshole. "You leave me and run right into his arms? You fucking whore."

Liz awoke in my arms and immediately showed an expression of terror. She squeezed me tightly with both of her hands.

"What are you doing here, Asshole?" I asked. "You shouldn't be here."

"I heard through the grapevine that you were banging my leftovers," Asshole said, stumbling and walking at the same time.

"You're drunk," Liz said, still gripping me in complete terror. "Go home Asshole."

[Reader's Note: Once again, she didn't refer to him as Asshole, but he's a fucking asshole!]

We were close enough to the door that I could get Liz inside and safe.

"Get inside, lock the door and call 911," I whispered.

She went inside and I closed the door behind her. Things were about to get really bad.

Chapter 9

The Asshole Strikes Back

Readers, this is what sucks about being the good guy. Sometimes you find yourself fighting for somebody's honor and sometimes you just have to knock out an asshole.

"I see through your little nice guy routine," Asshole said, each word slurring from his lips. "You wanted the little whore for yourself."

"You need to stop referring to her as a whore!" I yelled, firmly, with every last ounce of my body getting ready to rumble.

Asshole looked at me for a second and then proceeded over to my bushes and took a piss. Seriously, what the fuck? Asshole is by no means a push over either. He had to be at least six-foot-two and easily two-twenty. Every inch of him was leaning over my fucking bush.

"You think you are so fucking clever," Asshole said, while zipping his pants back up. "What Lizzy and I had was pure. It was fucking meant to last."

"This isn't the way to tell her this, man," I said, while starting to feel a little sorry for the asshole. "You need to go home and sober up. I will call you a cab."

Asshole seemed to ponder things for a brief moment. I thought a fight was going to be averted until his face started to show rage. It was the kind of thing paramedics see a lot.

"You know she fucking made me do it," he said, in a quiet and homicidal tone. "The bitch was always seeing other guys. You are just the latest fucking proof."

"So you hit her," I said, while getting pissed off. "That's your fucking answer. You never touch, hit, strike, or kick a woman."

Yeah, Asshole didn't like that response. He started to stumble in my direction.

"You need to relax," I said. "You need to back off of me right now!"

I remember looking behind me and I could see Liz's face in the window. She was on the phone and crying something fierce.

When I turned back around Asshole's fist was headed in my face's direction. I was able to move slightly, but he connected with my ear. At the time I didn't feel it at all. Later on, it hurt like a son of a bitch.

"Dude, what the fuck are . . . ." I said.

Asshole wasn't done yet, as he swung another hay maker in my direction. This time it wasn't a sucker punch, so I was able to block it and move away from him. I didn't want to return fire and risk hurting Liz or losing my job. Don't get me wrong, I wanted to thrash a beating on this guy, but I had to be the responsible one.

"Why aren't you fighting back?" He yelled. "Are you afraid? Did Liz run out and get herself a little pacifist pussy?"

In the distance I could hear sirens. It was most definitely a welcomed sound. I could tell Asshole was getting more and more out of control by the moment.

"Did she call the fucking cops?" He yelled, while flaring his arms around. "Great, you keep doing all of these awful things to me, bitch! Why the hell are you torturing me?"

"Asshole, you need to quiet down," I said, really just trying to keep him occupied as the police were approaching. "Liz isn't doing anything to you. She wants you to stay away from her."

As I uttered my last word, Asshole bum rushed me. I side stepped his drunken attempt and pushed him to the grass. The cops pulled in right after and I took a step in that direction. Asshole kicked out my back leg as I took my second step away from him. It made me pause for a second, long enough for him to jump on top of me. I was able to get my hands up to block most of the punches but he was able to land some hard knocks and bites before the cops pulled him off. Yes, the fucker beat me.

"He's the guy!" Liz yelled, while walking out of the house and crying. "He attacked my roommate and me."

Liz walked over to me and put my head up in her lap. I had received worse and honestly had given out much worse, but it was nice to have Liz fussing over me. At least that's what I remember thinking at the time. That was until Asshole left us with some parting words.

"Bitch, you will never be rid of me!" He said, while being put in the squad car. "This isn't fucking over."

Asshole kicked the window of the squad car as the door shut behind him. I could feel Liz trembling in fear. I looked up at her face and she tried to flash me a smile. Her tears were flowing down like a faucet.

Liz insisted on driving me to the emergency room. My ear was bleeding from one of his sucker punches, but other than that, I was doing just fine. She stayed with me and held my hand the entire time we were in the waiting room. Neither of us said a word. I had no idea what to say. I felt bad for her as I looked down into her beautiful eyes. They had turned gray, which she had said meant she was sad. It gets me down to think about Liz without her wonderful blue eyes.

The doctor checked me out and said I had a mild concussion. Liz shed a tear when she heard the news. She tugged at my hand to let go, but I held on tight.

"It's not that bad sweetie," I said, trying to sound reassuring. "I just have to be here for a couple of hours and then I can come home and bug you."

"You could never bug me," she said, with a smile.

Robert called me on my cell phone and told me he and his wife were in the lobby. Liz gladly told him were I was and now more people could see me in a backless gown.

"OMG. . . . are you okay?" January said, while walking right toward Liz. "Did that fuck wad hurt you?"

"How are you doing?" Robert said, while shaking my hand. "Anything I can do?"

"Um, can you bring Ian home?" Liz asked, in the direction of Robert. "He's not allowed to leave for a couple of hours and I want to go home and get it situated for his arrival. He shouldn't have to clean things up when he goes home."

"You shouldn't go back there by yourself," January said. "I will go with you."

Liz agreed and walked over to me to kiss my forehead. Just the feel of her lips on my forehead made my headache go away for a few seconds. I don't think she realized the power she had over me at that point.

"I will see you at home, my champion," Liz whispered, into my ear. "You are truly a wonderful man and you make me feel so special."

Liz and January walked out of the room and I thought things were going to be okay. We had made it through the incident still holding hands and that's all that mattered. Still, I was pissed I didn't hit the asshole!

"She seems to really care about you," Robert said, with a grin. "Plus she's smoking hot. Don't mess this one up."

"I really care about her," I replied. "I have no intentions of messing this up."

Robert drove me home a few hours later and helped me up to the door. My balance still wasn't the best at the moment. January had already left, but the living room light was still on and I could see Liz's outline. I opened the door and there were Liz's bags by the door.

"What the hell," I said, looking at Robert.

"I don't know man," Robert relied. "Do you want me to stick around?"

"No, thanks for bringing me this far," I said, while tapping him on the shoulder. "I'll call you tomorrow buddy."

Robert left and Liz came into view. She had a sad, distant look on her face. You could tell she had been crying for a while.

"I was hoping to be gone before you came home," she said, quietly. "I don't want to see you get hurt anymore over me."

"So you're just going to leave?" I said, probably a little too harshly, but my ear was sore.

Liz fell to the floor and started to cry. It crushed my heart into a million pieces. I didn't want to be mad and cause her more pain. I went over to her and sat down beside her. As I put my hand on her shoulder, she acted irritated and stood up suddenly.

"Maybe he's telling the truth and he'll just keep coming after me," Liz said, her body was shaking. "If you're in my life you will only be his target as well. You need to stay far away from me."

She headed back to her room and started to pack her last bag. I followed her into the bedroom.

"I don't want to stay away from you," I said. "Asshole isn't going to be the reason we break up. I can screw things up on my own thank you very much."

It was just for a moment, but I caught Liz trying to hide a smile. I turned Liz around toward me and kissed her. I truly cared for this woman. She was beautiful, charming, and so smart. I couldn't figure out why she didn't see us as perfect for each other.

"You're not going anywhere," I said, scared to death she was just going to tell me to fuck off. "This is your home. This is where you belong."

"I like you Ian!" She said, with a freaked out expression on her face. "I don't want to get my heart broken again."

"This has been one hell of a first date," I said, while smiling. "I'm looking forward to date number two."

"You're a silly, silly man," she said, with a grin. "Come over here."

Liz walked over to the bed. She made me lay down first. Then Liz began to slowly undress me, taking off my shoes and pants. She then turned off the bedroom light and curled up into my lap.

"What are we going to do about him?" Liz asked.

"First, we're going to file a restraining order and I have a few other ideas as well," I said, trying to sound reassuring. "You're safe for now. Close your eyes and try to get some sleep."

Through a court clerk friend of mine, I was able to get Liz a quick hearing in court to put the restraining order in play. It's truly amazing how many favors you can get from the courthouse, by simply sending them a few naughty pictures of yourself over Facebook. You are welcome ladies.

The hearing wasn't going to be pretty for either of us. Asshole had to be present and the last thing I wanted to do was put her in the same room with him. Still, Liz wanted to be there, even though her lawyer was the only one required in the courtroom for our side.

Liz was panicking from the moment she woke up that morning. She must have changed her clothes at least a dozen times. Her bedroom looked like a disaster area.

"Should I wear make-up to something like this?" She asked, before retreating back into the bathroom.

For the next hour, Liz did that over and over again. She asked me about her dress, her shoes, her hair and what temperature it might be in the courtroom. Every time I would attempt to answer, she just walked back into her room or the bathroom.

We arrived at the courthouse about an hour early and had a seat on a bench. She gave me her shaking hand to hold. I felt so bad she was going to have to confront him. I wasn't sure she was doing the right thing.

"You're going to be just fine," I said, while gently stroking her hair. "There is nothing he can do to you. Just remember, he's the asshole here."

"I just wish he didn't have to be here," she said, a single tear began to drip down her face. "What if he calls me a liar? What if the judge doesn't believe me?"

"Listen to me," I said, while gripping her face with both of my hands and looking deeply into her eyes. "I will be in there, so just look at me and don't even pay any attention to the Asshole. As for the judge, she will believe you because you're in the right here."

Before long, our lawyer showed up and it was time to head into the court room. We were inside for a few moments when Asshole came swaggering into the room. He was dressed in a suit, one that he probably had to steal.

The judge entered the room and had everybody sit down. She wanted to hear from Liz's lawyer first.

"If it pleases the court, my client would like to speak on her own behalf," our lawyer said.

Liz stood up from her chair. I give her credit for having the guts to stand up in front of a judge, but you could tell she was a hot mess. Every inch of her body was shaking and all the asshole could do was sit in his seat and snicker.

"Your honor, I just don't feel safe having him anywhere near me," Liz said, while trying to keep her emotions in check. "He has hit me on several occasions and attacked a friend of mine recently. He said he'd never quit coming after me."

The judge spent the next twenty minutes asking Liz about anything and everything regarding her relationship with Asshole. I was proud of the way she handled herself and kept her composure. Then the judge started to ask her about me. She wanted to know what kind of guy I was and if I provided a good living environment for her.

"Ian has done nothing but protect me, offer me a place to stay and listen to my problems," Liz said, as a few tears squeaked their way out. "I like and trust him very much."

"You can have a seat my dear," the judge said. "I want to hear from the roommate."

I wasn't expecting to get up in front of the judge and Liz's lawyer objected. The judge overruled her lawyer, so I stood up and answered questions about the night he attacked me. Asshole made coughing noises during my entire testimony.

"From the moment I met her, I felt protective over her," I said. "In the time that I've been privileged to know her, my protective instincts have only gotten stronger. Your honor, I truly care about this woman and I don't want to see any more harm come to her because of that man."

"Bullshit!" Asshole said. "He just wants to get into her pants like everybody else!"

"You will refrain from talking Mr. Asshole unless spoken to!" The judge said, with a harsh tone.

She had me sit back down and now it was Asshole's turn to get up and answer questions. I had to give it to him; he had rehearsed all of his answers very well. He was always careful to stop just short of blaming Liz for the beatings. He had a pleasant smile on his face and he didn't have anymore outbursts. Things were looking good for him until the judge asked him about confronting me at my house.

"She made me go there," Asshole said, starting to look out of sorts. "She wouldn't answer any of my calls. She just ended things."

"What happened the last time you two were together as a couple?" The judge asked.

"We had a fight," Asshole said, ever so quietly.

"Did you strike her?" The judge asked.

"It wasn't supposed to happen that way," Asshole said, anger showed all over his face. "We were supposed to be together forever. You fucking ruined us you bitch!"

Liz grabbed my leg. She was trembling and tears were flowing down her face. All I could do was sit there and it sucked. Somebody really needed to teach this fucker a lesson.

"I have made my decision," the judge said. "Mr. Asshole, you need to be taught how to treat a lady. Unfortunately I can't do that today, but I can grant this restraining order and that is exactly what I'm going to do."

"But your honor!" Asshole said.

"Don't you ever interrupt me!" The judge said. "You are to have no contact with her. You are not allowed to go within one mile of her home, work, or favorite hang-outs."

"Why am I being punished when she's being the bitch?" Asshole asked. "Now, I can't even go to my favorite hangouts. This is fucking bullshit."

"I've had enough of you, Mr. Asshole," the judge said, while pointing at her bailiff. "I'm finding you in contempt of court. Take him directly to jail."

The bailiff placed Asshole in cuffs and he was taken out of the room pissing and moaning.

"You will never be rid of me you bitch," Asshole said. "Fucking, never!"

I grabbed Liz's hand and helped her up. She was still trembling, but her tears had stopped flowing. I was quick to give her a hug and a smile to help calm her down.

"Is it all over?" She asked, very quietly.

"You won my dear," I said, while smiling. "You were absolutely wonderful. I'm so proud of you."

I wasn't convinced that was going to be the last time we'd see Asshole. Still, I had done what I could to protect her for now and all I wanted to do was get Liz out of this hell and go home and open a bottle of wine.

Chapter 10

Asking Her to Go Steady

Mid-May had come upon us and the weather was beautiful. Liz was still living in my place, but our relationship hadn't moved forward that much. Don't get me wrong, we would kiss multiple times each day. In fact, it was becoming a night time ritual of mine to kiss her before bed. She would also come into my bedroom in the middle of the night and curl up next to me.

Still, we hadn't really had that relationship conversation yet. Everything seemed to be happening backwards. I was already living with Liz and in a lot of ways we both acted like a couple around each other, but there was no physical contact past kissing and spooning.

"Why haven't you two had the talk yet?" Robert asked, while sitting in my kitchen.

"We've just both been busy, I guess," I said, not really believing what I was saying. "Between the court case, both of our jobs and . . . . we just haven't."

"Ian, do you like this girl?" Robert said.

"You know I do," I replied, sounding agitated.

"Well then, get out of your head and make a move," Robert said. "Maybe, she's waiting on you to make this a relationship. Sex aside, you two already seemed like a couple."

Robert would go on to challenge my manhood and tease me for a while longer. He was right. I needed to make the next move and I had an idea. So, I called Liz at her restaurant and asked her out on a date for later that evening. Readers, I swear I heard her voice smile when she said yes. Is that even possible?

Liz came home from work right after dinner prep at her restaurant. She had been working since 8 A.M., but she seemed determined to stay in a good mood.

"Just give me, like, 30 minutes," Liz said, while walking into her bedroom.

For the next hour I sat on my couch watching television. Liz spent that time racing room-to-room like Taz from the Looney Tunes. It was so cute watching her mutter to herself while she was getting ready. Every 15 minutes or so, she would peek her head out of the door.

"I'm almost ready," she would say, while flashing me her smile. "It will be worth it. I promise."

Liz finally came out of the bathroom. She put one of her arms on the door and posed, so I could see every last detail of her hard work.

"What do you think?" She asked.

I told her to dress casual for the occasion. She had on a tank top and a black skirt. It was casual, but she looked amazing. Her hair was put up, exposing her sexy neck. She didn't have very much make-up on, but she was wearing this intoxicating scent. It would be a smell that I would learn to love and hold closely to my heart, but I digress.

"Wow," I said, while making sure to take in the whole package. "You are a beautiful, beautiful girl."

Liz flashed me her smile and seemed to blush a little bit. Liz was a fan of being doted upon, but at the same time, she always blushes when I do compliment her.

Everything about her seemed so easy to begin our evening. This was going to be the night that I would make her my girlfriend.

"So, where are you taking me?" She asked.

"It has been a while since I took a ride with a pretty girl on a Ferris wheel," I said.

"You mean?" She replied.

"I thought we would go downtown and ride the Ferris wheel," I replied. "Then, maybe walk around and grab something to eat."

Liz walked over to me and planted a kiss on my lips. Every time she would get that close to me, the greatest feeling in the world would dance up and down my spine. She is fucking amazing.

"Lead the way, my handsome man," Liz said, as she grabbed my arm and we left the house.

It's a short drive from our place to downtown. The sun had just made its way below the horizon when we made it to the Ferris wheel. It was a pretty night. The air wasn't too hot and Liz had her hand in mine as we waited our turn in line. Soon, we made our way onto the ride and lifted off.

"So, you said there was something we needed to talk about," Liz said.

"Did I say that?" I replied, trying to play coy.

Liz lightly punched me in my arm. She then leaned over and kissed me.

"You can tell me," she said, while flashing her sad face.

I motioned at the ride operator as we passed by. You see, if you offer him a bribe, he's more than willing to stop the ride when you are at the very top. It just so happens you can see all of Tulsa from the top from there. When Liz and I reached the top, the ride stopped. Imagine that.

"We started out doing things backwards," I said, thinking about every word I said before it left my head. "We started living together and then we had our first date."

"Do you not like where things are heading?" She asked, with a sad look on her face.

I pulled a jewelry box out of my pocket. Readers, my entire body was shaking.

"I'm saying this all wrong," I replied, while handing her the box. "You make me happy every single day that I get a chance to see you. I guess what I'm trying to say is . . . ."

Liz opened up the box to find a necklace inside. On the chain was a tear drop diamond.

"It's absolutely beautiful," she said, as she examined her new trinket.

"I may sound corny, but I want you to be my girlfriend," I said, while taking the necklace out of the box and placing it around her neck. "I want you to be able to look at the necklace and feel safe. It will be my mission to make sure you never shed a tear because of me."

Honestly, that goal of mine didn't last very long, because a tear drop started to slowly move down her cheek. Liz put both of her hands on my face and kissed me.

"You're a good man," she said. "I always feel safe and special when I'm around you. Of course, I will be your girlfriend."

Within moments of her reply, the Ferris wheel was moving again. We went around in a circle a few more times before our turn came to an end. As we were getting off, Liz grabbed my hand and pressed it tightly.

"I want to tell you something," she said, an embarrassed look popped up on her face. "Oh, now's probably not the time."

"No, tell me," I said, very much curious.

"All good things to those who wait," Liz replied, with a grin on her face. "I will tell you soon. I promise."

Liz kissed me one last time before we started to walk around downtown. The kiss was passionate and ended with me tilting her head backwards into a dip.

"I hope you know what you mean to me," Liz said, as I raised her back up.

We made our way back home just after midnight that evening. Readers, the night had been amazing. After the Ferris wheel, we just wondered around and talked. I could have walked with her all night.

"Do you want me to open some wine?" I asked, walking into the kitchen.

"That sounds delightful," Liz said, while heading toward her room. "Pour me a small glass. I will be right out."

So, I opened up a very nice Merlot and poured two glasses. Liz still hadn't come out of her room, so I went into the living room and sat in my chair. I turned on the television, but . . . .

"Hey, turn that TV off!" She yelled, still behind her closed door.

Okay, cool, she wants to talk some more. Maybe she'll come out and she'll just lay down on me and drink some wine. Hmm, she's taking her sweet time. Is she fixing up her make-up for me? No, she wasn't really wearing any tonight.

While I was busy in my head, I didn't really notice that music had started to play in the background. Then the living room lights went dim. Liz walked into the living room holding a lit candle in her hand.

"What's going . . . . you look . . . ." I said, words honestly escaped me.

"No talking my dear," Liz said, in the sexiest of tones. "Just sit back and enjoy."

I examined Liz from her beautiful face, right down to her sexy painted toes. She had on sexy red heels and black, fucking sexy stockings that fix perfectly over her silky, smooth white legs. The only other thing adorning her magnificent body was a black corset, accompanied by tiny little pink bows skipping down the middle. As

Colleen Michaels

my eyes made their way up and down her body, Liz started to dance slowly, seductively.

"Are you sure you're ready?" I asked.

Liz stopped dancing and stuck her finger up at me. She then dipped that finger in my wine glass and brushed it along her lips. Then she pressed that finger along my lips and leaned in close to my ear.

"No talking," she whispered, gently kissing my ear in the process. "Just watch."

Liz grabbed the disc changer remote and selected a song.

"Oh, perfect," Liz said. "This is a very sexy song."

Liz slowly turned the music up and began to dance within inches of me. She turned around exposing her perfectly shaped ass and grabbed a nearby wooden chair. As the music hit its chorus, Liz began to dance up and down on the chair. She did nothing quickly, preferring to accentuate every spine tingling move that she made.

As the song progressed, I could feel myself really liking what I saw. I've never had the balls to ask her, but I think Liz did as well. She moved the chair and crawled in my direction, making sure to lip sink every word being said in the song. Liz crawled up my lap and lightly brushed her luscious lips against mine. It might have been the greatest feeling of my life.

"Do you like what you see?" she whispered, before kissing my lips again.

"Very much," I replied, barely getting it out of my throat.

"Good," she said, with her wicked grin racing across her face. "Now watch."

Liz ran her lips up and down my neck, gently kissing as she went. Her right leg rubbed up against the inside of my leg. By that point, Liz definitely knew I was pleased with her performance. She looked up at me and smiled. Liz took her leg and started to rub it against my privates. It felt so good and I so wanted her at that point. I couldn't take it anymore, so I tried to touch her body. Liz wasn't having any of it, putting my hands behind my back.

"Not yet," she whispered.

Liz then rubbed her hands under my shirt and then down into my pants. It was amazing watching her in perfect rhythm with the music. She looked like a sex goddess and on that night I was living in the clouds.

As the song ended, Liz got up in my lap and we began to rub up against each other. I hadn't had dry sex since high school film class, but we played beautiful music together. When the last note played, Liz turned the disc player off.

"Now?" I asked, really, really hoping the answer was yes.

Liz got up off my lap and let out a little laugh. She then grabbed my shirt and pulled me up.

"Now, handsome," she said.

That was my cue and I jumped to the challenge. I picked her up and carried her into my bedroom. Liz just let go and let me place her down on my bed. She looked amazing starring up at me with those sparkling eyes.

"Do you have protection?" She asked. "Because I have condoms in my room I can go get?"

I opened my drawer next to the bed and grabbed a couple. I kissed her, slowly moving down her neck.

"Don't worry about it," I said, while landing at her hard nipples. "I have a couple."

As I opened the condom, I made sure to devote ample time to licking and nibbling at her nipples. She seemed to like it, as frequencies only heard by certain sea creatures blared from her mouth.

I finally had the condom in place and we fucked. It was our first time together, but we both took advantage of the opportunity to explore each others bodies. She was magnificent, doing what ever she was told and dishing out a few orders herself. I couldn't get past how beautiful she looked and how soft and wonderful she felt. Then it happened. Liz's body began to shake, she got loud, and an explosion of perfection occurred. During the course of the next couple of hours, we both had more than one explosion. Readers, I'm sorry for the TMI, but it was necessary to reveal to you just how happy I was at this point.

When neither of us could take it anymore, Liz fell into my arms. Her naked, cool body felt wonderful against my warm skin.

"You make me crazy happy," Liz whispered, into my ear, before looking into my eyes and smiling.

"You were amazing," I whispered back, goose bumps were covering my body like a coat. "You are amazing in so, so many ways."

Liz and I laid in each others arms for a while, with neither of us saying a word. I could tell by the look on her face that she had something to say. I happened to be correct for once.

"You remember that thing I was going to tell you and then I chickened out?" Liz said, while covering her face in embarrassment.

"Yes," I said, while looking at her cute freckles. "You can tell me. You can tell me anything."

Liz took her hands off her face. She kissed me deeply, while never taking her gaze off my eyes.

"I think I love you," she said, looking nervous while waiting for any response from me.

It didn't take very long. I had been feeling the same way for days now.

"I think I love you too, pretty, pretty girl," I said. "You make me happy and that's big for me. I love you, too."

Liz's face lit up like New Orleans during Mardi Gras. She put her hands on my face and kissed me one last time.

"I think I will use you as my pillow tonight," she said, while getting comfortable on my mid-section.

After a few minutes, Liz fell asleep. I was tired, but how I could I sleep after a night like this one. So, I stayed up and watched her sleep for a while.

Chapter 11

One Happy Fucking Family

S o, I was in love. It's amazing, after Julie, I never
thought that would be possible again. Liz and I
were in love and in lust pretty much 24/7.

We both worked at night, so our schedules matched
up perfectly. I would get home 30 minutes before she
would, so she'd text me before leaving work and I
would have a glass of wine, a beer, or my open arms
waiting for her when she arrived home.

On that particular evening, I received a text from
my roommate about wanting to take a bubble bath. So,
when Liz arrived home that night, I had a bubble bath
waiting for her. She slipped out of her smelly restaurant
clothes, kissed my neck twice and slid right into the tub.
I took a seat right next to the tub, which allowed us to
be at the same eye level.

"What time is it?" Liz asked.

"Just after two-thirty," I replied.

"Good, we have time," She said, I think more for
her own benefit. "I can't sleep all morning though. You
can't let me sleep all morning."

Her face was like a deck of cards and it was tipping off her nervousness. Liz's eyes would try to lock onto mine, but then she would look away.

"Is everything okay, sweetie?" I asked.

"Yeah, I'm fine," she replied, suddenly her face lit up like she had just figured out the meaning of life. "I have a question for you."

"Ask your question," I replied, starting to get a little nervous myself by her behavior.

"My family wants to meet you," she whispered, while immediately putting her hands over her face. "Is that okay?"

"Why don't you invite them over to dinner this weekend," I replied.

"Yay!" Liz said, while reaching over the rub and stealing a kiss. "Get in the tub, handsome man."

I took off my clothes, forgetting all about my socks and jumped in the bubble bath with her. Liz just kept her eyes locked on mine and smiled.

"I love you," she said. "You make me laugh every single day."

Liz reached over and things started to get hot and heavy. Readers, from there I will skip the intimate details of our bubble bath adventure, but I will tell you the things you should know. First, I was amazing in that tub. We're talking major league production here boys and girls. Second, it was now close to three-thirty in the morning and she was yelling louder than a holler monkey. I was so sure the cops were going to be called due to the noise. Third, I was the man!

"You were amazing," Liz said, while sliding back into the tub and grinning.

It was the morning of the family dinner and I got up early to hit the grocery store. I was making supper for Liz's mother, sister, and uncle. Her uncle, Brad, had been living at her mom's house since the whole suicide incident. Liz said he had always kind of been a part of the immediate family. I believe she said he was a family dork with a hair piece.

So, I spent entirely too long at the store and returned home with three weeks worth of groceries for one meal. Liz had the music jacked up and she was dancing around the living room. She didn't hear me come in, so she continued around the room with the grace of a butterfly. Readers, it's a pretty good feeling to be in love with and crushing on the same girl.

The song ended and a slow one began, so I seized the opportunity to dance with my lady. I grabbed her hand and spun her around.

"You make me have butterflies in my stomach," Liz said, while putting her head on my shoulder.

"I got enough food to feed an army," I said, enjoying the moment. "Are we ready for tonight?"

Liz looked up at me and smiled. As usual the room became a little brighter when she flashed me her gold ribbon smile.

"We are absolutely ready for tonight," Liz said, before standing on my feet and kissing me.

I felt confident that Liz was right. So what that her uncle might suck. I already knew her sister seemed cool from that night at the house. I was pretty certain Liz's mom had to be pretty great since she raised the woman that I loved. I couldn't know for sure, because Liz never really talked about them much. I would bring it up, but she would always change the subject.

Liz's family arrived together and 10 minutes early. My darling was still changing for like the 30th time, so I answered the door and played entertainer. I was also cooking dinner at that point, so yeah, it sucked right from the beginning.

Her sister Amy walked right over to me and planted a big kiss on my cheek. She then handed me her purse.

"You look as good as I remember," Amy said, while licking her lips. "Do me a favor and put my purse in the closet."

Amy was a cute girl, but I was impressed that I really didn't find her to be all that appealing anymore. I saw that she licked her lips a lot like Liz does, but it just wasn't nearly as intoxicating or refined.

"Can I get anybody something to drink?" I said.

"Yes, do you have any Scotch?" Uncle Brad asked. "I would love one if you got it."

"No heavy drinking," Liz's mom, Debbie said. "You need to drive home tonight."

"Oh, relax yourself, I'm only going to have a couple," the uncle replied.

Liz finally came out of her room and greeted her family. She was dressed up in a very pretty, long dark gray dress. You'd think I would have gotten used to her beauty by then, but she took my breath away.

"There you are," Debbie said, with a frown on her face. "I don't remember raising my kids to not greet their guests when they arrive."

"I'm sorry Mom," Liz said, her smile faded away and was replaced by a faked attempt. "I'm glad you all could make it tonight."

"Well, we had to see what you were doing with yourself ever since what's his name?" Debbie said. "Honestly, I don't understand why you didn't just come home."

"Mom, now's not the time to talk about this," Liz said, her face looked miserable.

I had escaped to the kitchen after Liz had arrived, but I could hear the whole conversation. After just moments of listening to their conversation I could already see why Liz never brought them up much. So, I returned to the living room to save my beautiful girl.

"Okay, dinner is ready," I said, to a tension filled room.

I had hoped eating would put an end to the bickering, but I was wrong. Over a giant bowl of spaghetti, Liz's family had a throw down. Each person took turns downing glasses of wine while informing my girlfriend just how disappointed they were in her.

"I have to live with Mom by myself," Amy said. "Why do I have to be the one that has to deal with her all the time since Dad's death?"

"Shut up Amy," Uncle Brad slurred. He had been shit faced drunk just five minutes into dinner. "What your sister is trying to say is your mom could use the company and you could use your family."

Readers, all of these were being said right in front of me. I was sitting at the mother fucking table. Yet, her mother, uncle, and sister kept firing one missile after another at both Liz and I.

"Honestly, Liz, your bad choice of a boyfriend attacks you and you choose Ian over your own family?" Debbie said. "And Ian, you allow her to do this. The good Lord already took my husband away from me and what, you're trying to take my oldest daughter away as well?"

"Mom!" Liz yelled, while getting up from the table. "Why are you doing this? We are happy and wanted you to come over and see that I'm doing well."

Debbie took a tissue out of her purse and rubbed her eyes. Amy was texting somebody and Uncle Brad had just finished his fifth glass of wine. Liz looked absolutely miserable.

"Well, I guess you no longer need us then," Debbie said, sounding very fucking condescending. "I've lost my appetite. Brad are you good to drive?"

"I think so, sure," Brad said, with a belch.

"Um, that's probably not a good idea," I said, while grabbing his keys and then mine.

"Well, Amy doesn't have her license, so, what should we do then Sherlock?" Brad said. "I'm older than you and I think I know when I'm okay to drive."

Tears started forming in Liz's eyes and it crushed my heart. She quickly walked into her room and closed the door hard behind her. I guess it was up to me to be the good guy, again.

"I will give you a ride home," I said, while ushering the family out of my house. "We can bring your car back to you later."

I took one last glance at Liz's door and I could hear music playing in her room before I left the house. I felt so very sorry for Liz. I really, really did.

Driving the family home was no picnic either. Uncle Brad was passed out in the back seat next to Amy. Debbie was in the front seat starring daggers into the windshield.

"I don't understand Liz," Amy said. "There is always so much drama with her. Plus, she thinks she's too good for her own family."

"Hush Amy," Debbie said. "You know she has a problem. I'm sure she's still blaming it on us as well.

"Is there a problem?" I asked.

"Do you not know about Liz's condition?" Amy asked, while laughing out loud.

"Shocking, she didn't tell you," Debbie said. "This is why she should be living with us. After what happened with . . . . I can't believe she's acting this way."

I pulled into the South Tulsa neighborhood where Liz's family lived. It was a completely different scene than the last time I had been there for Liz's dad. Still, each time was equally dramatic.

"You see, Liz was diagnosed as Bi-polar," Debbie said, while putting her arm on mine. "She needs to be with people who know how to handle her condition. Liz needs her family."

Amy helped Uncle Brad get out of the car. They both made there way to the house while Debbie stayed behind. At this point, Debbie once again had a tissue out and was drying off tears. She is such a fucking drama queen!

"Liz chose to come and live with me," I said, trying to stay calm. "She seems to be happy. I can promise you she's safe and I will do everything I can to keep her that way."

I'm pretty sure Debbie wasn't even listening to me. If she had been then she dismissed it right away.

"What happens when she has her dark days?" Debbie said. "You have no idea how Liz gets when she refuses to take her medicine."

The flood gates just flew open for Debbie from there. I had no idea what to do. Debbie jumped out of the vehicle and began to walk up her drive-way bawling. I got out behind her and followed her to the door. Again, I didn't know what else to do.

"You know what, I don't care anymore," Debbie said, while standing in her doorway. "She's your fucking problem now. I can't handle loosing another one."

Before I could get another word out, Debbie shut the door behind her. I was left standing like an idiot on my girlfriend's mother's porch. I was confused, but I decided it was time to go home and check on Liz.

I arrived to an empty house. Liz had left a note for me on my bed explaining they needed her at the restaurant. Her room was a mess, so I almost missed the note. Liz's clothes were everywhere; something not normal for my normally very neat girlfriend. Even her nightstand looked like a tornado had just made a pass and knocked over her lamp.

I went into her bathroom and it was also a disaster area. I'm not a big fan of snooping, but something inside me told me to do it anyways. So, I went over to her medicine cabinet and started reading labels. She had two full bottles of one prescription. I hadn't heard of this particular drug and I noticed the fill dates were from a couple months back. So, I jumped online and sadly my suspicions had been correct.

Not sure at that point what my next move should be, I tried calling Liz. Unfortunately, my call went straight to her voicemail. She never turns her phone off at work in case of emergencies. I knew she probably just wanted to have some alone time at work. Still, I decided to make the trip up to her restaurant. I had to know that she was all right.

Readers, this ended up being a very bad idea. I probably should have stayed home.

Chapter 12

I'll Take a Woman Scorned to Go

B y the time I got to the restaurant it had been closed for a couple of hours. There were two cars in the parking lot. I went up to the door and the bartender was still inside. He recognized me and was cool enough to come over and let me in the doors.

"She's in the back," the bartender said. "She's not doing so well."

"Thank you," I said.

I went into the back room and right away I could hear her crying. She had her legs pinned up under her chin. Her office was the size of a large dog kennel, so space was limited. Still, she was obviously in a sad position and it was killing me to see her in that manner.

Not really sure what to do, I went into her office and put my arm around her. She seemed surprised at first, but soon she just laid her head on me.

"So, that was my loving family," Liz said, it was hard to make out everything she was saying through her crying. "Did my mother tell you?"

"She said a lot," I said. "She said you are Bi-Polar. She said your father suffered from the same problem."

Liz looked up at me and all of her self-confidence had escaped from her face. She looked defeated and in need of somebody to tell her everything was going to be okay. On that night, I wasn't that person. I could have made things better by just shutting the fuck up, but I kept pushing.

"Your mom is worried you're not taking your medication," I said. "Have you been taking your medicine?"

"Yes, I've been taking my medicine," Liz said, very quietly. "This isn't something you should be worried about."

Readers, I didn't have much room to talk. I take medication for my depression every single day. Sometimes, I forget and my friends and family can tell right away. So, I truly understand what Liz is going though. Still, she just lied straight to my face.

"I cleaned up your room," I said, watching her face for any kind of reaction. "I might have read something important to you. Don't be mad."

That expression I was waiting for turned out to be one of fear and shock. Liz stood up and began to head toward the exit. She pulled a cigarette from her ear and lit one up in the back alley.

"Tell me you didn't read my journal," she said, with a look of desperation on her face.

I couldn't tell her that and by the look on her face she didn't want to hear otherwise. I had managed to trap myself in an alley with an angry girl and a relationship that was worsening by the moment. Yet, I kept moving forward with the conversation. Boy was I an idiot!

"You wrote that you weren't taking your meds anymore," I said. "That you hadn't taken them in a while. Believe me I know how important it is to take them."

Liz took a really long drag from her cigarette. Her face was full of rage.

"You read my fucking journal," she said. "How dare you read my most personal thing that I have without my fucking permission! Ian, I thought I could trust you."

Liz threw her cigarette onto the ground and stomped it out. She went over to the exit door and dropped to her knees. Liz had her hands over her face.

"I was worried about you," I said, while slowly moving my way over to her. "I care about you. I know I shouldn't have done that."

"Oh, so now you just care about me," Liz said, her tears were getting worse by the second. "I guess you don't love me anymore. Now that you know I'm a crazy girl."

I sat down and tried to hold her hand. Liz moved her hand quickly and I could make out a large cut on her arm. I slowly moved up her shirt and found several cuts I had never noticed before.

"What did you do?" I asked, while looking at her arm.

Liz covered her arm and stood up. She wiped her eyes and now had a pissed off look on her face.

"Yes, I'm completely screwed up," she said, while walking around in no apparent direction. "You don't want to love somebody like me. I'm really fucking sorry."

Liz started to jog toward the parking lot. I probably should have let her go, perhaps she would have cooled off. Instead, I followed her out to her car. She was at her driver's side door and was frantically trying to find her keys in her purse.

"Go away, Ian," Liz said, while not taking her eyes off her purse. "You are better off without me."

"I don't want to lose you," I said. "You mean too much to me."

I grabbed Liz's face with both of my hands and kissed her. It was slow, passionate, and wonderful. It was the only thing I could think to do. For a moment, Liz seemed to let go and allowed herself to enjoy the moment. Still, that moment didn't last for very long.

"You never really had me," Liz said, while trying not to look directly into my eyes. "I was never good enough for you."

Liz found her keys, got in her car, and took off down the road. I stood there staring at her car until it disappeared out of my life or so I thought at the time.

Not really sure what to do next, I wondered around Tulsa. I didn't want to go home. Liz might be there and she obviously didn't want to see me. Then it occurred to me, she might never be in my place again. I might never know that wonderful feeling of having her come into my bedroom and curl up beside me ever again. That feeling made me throw up a little inside my mouth.

So, with no where else to go, I parked my car at the house and walked down the street to the nearby park Liz and I strolled to once upon a time. The sun would be coming up in a couple of hours, but at that point it was pitch dark out and I was the only one outside in the silence.

I took a seat on one of the swings and began to become lost in my head. Maybe she was right and we were never meant to be. After all, when you add our crazies together, it might just be too much to work. It might just be too much of a hurdle to overcome. Nope, I refused to believe that. God took Julie away from me. I refused to believe he would send Liz into my life just to fuck with me.

It was so quiet outside, but my mind was so loud. The swing was acting as a crutch for my nervous energy, but I needed something stronger for my head. Readers, the thing I was most worried about was I didn't think I had the energy to get through having my heart broken again.

I had been outside for almost two hours and the sun was starting to peak its head over the horizon. So, I pulled out my last cigarette, lit it up slowly, and began to walk home. I had no idea what I was going to find once I arrived. The trip felt like I was a dead man walking or something. My head was going over every scenario I was possibly going to face.

When I reached the house her car was in the driveway. This could have been a good sign. Maybe, she really just needed time to cool off or maybe she was waiting for me and would bitch me out once again.

I opened the door and she was waiting for me in the kitchen. She was wearing her large, frumpy bath robe. Liz did not appear to be happy.

"I saw your car in the drive-way," she said, very quietly.

"Yeah, I took a walk over to the park," I said.

"I'm sorry," she said, while standing up and taking off her robe. "I'm so, so sorry."

Liz wasn't wearing anything underneath her robe. She stood there exposing her beautiful body to me and to top it off she had my favorite smile on her face. It was truly an amazing sight to see. She did have leg warmers over her arms, probably to keep my mind off her problem. Still, at that moment, I thought one issue at a time.

"I want you to make love to me," she said, while biting the lower part of her lip. "I want to show you how much you mean to me."

Liz walked over to me and we began to kiss. I picked her up and carried her toward her room.

"No," she said. "Take me to your bed. Make me yours."

Not giving it a second thought, I reversed course and laid Liz down on my bed. For the next hour we made love. It was slow. It was deliberate. It was really fucking sensual. There was no dirty talk. There was no ass slapping. There was however the sounds of two people making beautiful magic together. Plus, we would slip in the love word from time-to-time.

Readers, the session ended with the both of us collapsing in pure bliss.

After a few minutes, Liz stood up and began to leave the room. She appeared to be happy. I had no idea. I didn't think love making was going to be in the cards. What the hell did I know?

"Where are you going?" I asked, while still waiting for most of my blood to return to my head from my lower regions.

"You get some rest," she said, in a very sweet tone. "I have something I need to get done but don't worry. I will return to your arms when I'm done."

Liz flashed me one more smile before leaving the room. I soaked it in and then turned over and went to bed. I would like to say all of my dreams were about her, but I can't control what I dream about. I'm pretty sure I dreamed about playing soccer against dinosaurs or something along those lines.

I awoke to my alarm clocking going off around 2 P.M. I had to work in a couple of hours, but I still had time to hang with Liz before we both went to our jobs. So, I got my ass out of bed and headed for the shower. I didn't hear Liz or music as I went into the bathroom, but didn't give it a second thought.

After getting ready for the day I headed out to the kitchen. It was still quiet. Perhaps, Liz was in her room? I knocked on the door and received no answer. So, I slowly opened her door expecting to see a sleeping beauty in the bed.

"No fucking way," I said, talking to myself.

There was nothing left in Liz's room. She had cleaned out her closet, her drawers and every thing else. I stood in her door way just starring at its emptiness. She was gone.

In shock I walked out to the kitchen. I started to look around for a note and I checked my cell for voice messages or texts. From there, I went online to check my e-mail and social media websites. I still found no messages from Liz. There are too many fucking things to check!

Irritated, upset, and completely devastated, I walked back into my room. Sitting right next to my alarm clock, the place where I had started my day, laid an envelope with my name on the front. I opened it up and it was a letter from Liz.

"My darling Ian,

I love you so very, very much.

I know it makes no sense, but it's that love I have for you that is the reason I have to leave. It's not fair for you to have to keep saving me from everything in my life.

My dad was Bi-Polar and he ended up killing himself. After what happened to Julie, I don't want you to ever have to worry about losing another girl that you love.

I'm in a bad place right now and I need to be able to solve this on my own. I need to make myself worthy of you. I just don't know how long it's going to take.

You are the only person who seems to understand what I'm going through. So, I beg you not to come after me. I plead for you to respect my wishes and know that you've already saved me. I was lost before you found me, rescued me and kept me safe.

Every moment that we shared together in this house has meant everything to me. I know I don't always express that fact, but you have been my guardian angel. Ian, you have very much been my hero and have helped me feel safe.

I truly hope last night won't be the last time we will ever make love, but unfortunately I can't make that promise. My goal is to get better and then return to your arms. I just don't know how long it will take.

I don't expect you to wait for me. Ian, please don't wait for me. You are such a good man and I know you will be a wonderful husband and an amazing father one day for some really lucky girl. You're a handsome, generous, loving, and kind man. I will never forget you or the love I have in my heart for you.

Ian, you are the love of my life.

I will miss you and Ibaka. Good bye my love.

Liz <3"

Readers, I fell to my bed and began to weep like a little girl. My heart had once again been smashed into a million pieces. I starred at the note until it was time to head towards work. The entire time, I was willing the words on the page to change. I was checking the letter for . . . . I don't know what I was looking for, but I never found it anyways.

All I could think was this had to be my fault. There had to be reason bad things kept happening to me when it came to my love life. I had to have done something so fucking wrong at some point in my life to warrant this punishment.

Chapter 13

I'm too Old for Break-ups

Readers, the thing that sucks about growing up and being dumped is you can't do the things you did as a college student. It seemed lame to sit in my room all day and sulk with the Counting Crows playing loudly in the background. You can't really prank call the ex because her cell phone had caller ID and it turned out there are stalker laws. I also remember making a mixed tape or two back in the day. I wonder if that ever works for anybody? I guess if you're a musician it might. Still, burning her a mixed CD just seemed silly.

"I've had those thoughts in my head for a month now," I said, while taking a bite of my tuna melt.

"Has it been a month, already," Robert said, while rolling his eyes. "I would have never of guessed."

It had been a month since Liz walked away. Robert had been great helping me get through my shit. Readers, before you start calling me a wuss you have to understand I council him on his wife all of the time. So, I guess you can say we're both just over dramatic women trapped in a muscular man's body. Well, I'm definitely a cut guy. Robert has been slacking off since he married January.

"So, you're saying no more sulking in the bedroom?" Robert said, with a grin on his face.

"I haven't been in my bedroom that much thinking about Liz," I said.

"Dude, if I hear 'Mr. Jones' one more time," Robert replied, while laughing out loud.

Okay, so maybe I had been reverting back to my teenage years a little bit. For about a week after Liz left, I pretty much didn't leave my room except for work and to let the dog out. I think I lost like 15 pounds that week since the kitchen either seemed far away or just not appealing. Robert came over on day five to rescue me with food and to check if I had been taking my pills. Being depressed on top of suffering from depression is so much fun—or not.

"Oh and remember how I had to stop you from calling her restaurant all those times," Robert said, while continuing to laugh. "Dude, you're such a stalker."

"I didn't try to call her that much," I said, while my face was becoming bright red. "I can't call her cell. She'd know it was me."

Robert didn't know the whole story with me trying to call Liz's restaurant. I thought about going over there, but I didn't want to be like Asshole. So, I called over there a couple of times. The bartender answered all 20 times and yes, I didn't say a word. On the 21st call, the bartender said something back to me.

"Ian, Liz hasn't been here in a couple of weeks," he said. "She's taking a leave of absence. She was hurting pretty bad."

"Thanks, man" I said, quietly into the phone.

"For what it's worth . . . . she really loved you," the bartender said. "She's just going through something right now."

I mumbled something back to him and hung up the phone. A sense of shame rushed over my body. It had been my intention to make Liz's life better. Perhaps, I had just made this worse.

"The funniest thing you've done so far is your attempt at making a mixed CD," Robert said, with a large smile on his face.

"I did no such thing," I said, while taking a swig from a wine bottle sitting next to me.

"You totally did," Robert replied, quickly. "Sure, you were wasted, but don't tell me you don't remember. I think every love song written in the '90s was in your CD player that night."

"Not every one," I said.

I had been drinking a lot for me since the break-up. There was one evening in particular that I upgraded from wine to Vodka and then got really pathetic. I spent like an hour in her room just sitting there and thinking about how I could get her back. One of those ideas was to make her a fucking CD. When Robert rolled by that evening I had laid out CDs all over my floor. To be fair at that point I had already moved on from making Liz a CD. Readers, I was drunk, so what do you want from me?

"I think it's time you get back out of the house," Robert said. "You need to meet somebody else or at least have some fun. Why don't you break out that little black book of yours?"

There is no little black book. Well, not since God created contacts in cell phones anyways. I hadn't really been thinking about other girls. Still, maybe Robert was right.

"Maybe I'll call somebody," I said. "It's the weekend. I wouldn't mind getting out and having some fun."

Robert had to go home and bow at January's feet or whatever, so I decided to make some plans for myself. I called my very favorite MILF. I called Kate. She was more than happy to hear from me. I had kind of gone away from her life in previous periods, so she had no problem coming over to my place that night.

It had been a while since I had seen another woman besides Liz. Part of me was ready to leave her behind. I had my own crazies to worry about. It could be a lot, at times, having to deal with her crazies as well. Kate is a very sexy woman. Maybe I'm not supposed to have anything serious in my life. I can just think about me and see gorgeous women like Kate when ever the need arises.

Kate arrived around 10 P.M. She was wearing a sexy summer dress. Her hair was held up with a pencil and she was wearing her sexy framed glasses. The beauty of Kate, she was always consistently sexy and cute. She worked out more than most college girls between going to the gym, raising her kid and having her fat lard of a husband laying on top of her all of the time. That's just creepy to think about.

"It has been a while," Kate said, while stretching out her long arms across the door. "I've missed you."

Readers, she looked very good, but I wasn't thinking about her at all. All I could think about was how Liz used to enter a room when she wanted to be noticed. She could make anything look or seem sexy. Kate was great, but she wasn't Liz. Still, Liz was gone, so I forced myself.

"I missed you," I said, pretending to smile. "I'm glad you're here. Can I get you a glass of wine?"

"Of course," Kate said, while flashing a smile. "Don't fill it up all the way. You know how I can get when I'm drunk."

Kate had been over for like two minutes and I already knew I could have sex that night. Normally, that feeling would be both expected and wanted, but things were different.

I gave Kate her wine glass and motioned her over to the living room. My disc player was on random and I just felt out of sorts. I sat down in my chair instead of the couch in hopes there would be a fair amount of distance between Kate and I.

"Why aren't you sitting on the couch?" Kate asked, while flashing her sad face.

Instead of sitting on the couch or anywhere else, Kate decided to sit on my chair's arm. She's tall so she had to lean over to speak with me. It seemed more awkward than anything else. After bullshitting about her family, she leaned over and we kissed. I was a bit startled at first, but I let go and decided to enjoy the experience.

"I've missed your lips," Kate said.

She got on her knees to make kissing a little less of a difficult task. Kate is a wonderful kisser and I was having fun. I guess I was having fun. I'm almost positive I was having fun at that point.

Kate then reached under my shirt and began to run her hands across my chest. This was definitely going in the direction of sex in the living room. I pulled her arms up and took of her shirt. She was wearing a very sexy black lace bra.

"You look and feel so good," I said, trying to find my inner player again.

Everything was going great. Things were getting hot and heavy. Hands were going anywhere and everywhere.

"Let's go to your room," Kate said, with a sexy grin.

"I'm right behind you," I said, grabbing her hand.

We headed toward my room, stopping to kiss along the way. We got to the door and her phone rang. We stopped what we were doing and she checked her phone.

"Oh, it's my husband," she said. "Please be quiet for a second."

So, she talked on the phone for a few minutes and I prepared my room for play time. By the time she got off the phone, I was waiting at my bedroom door.

"I'm sorry," she said, while walking up to me and running her leg across my crotch. "No more interruptions. I promise."

Kate was very good at changing modes very quickly. She could go from mommy, to wife to sexy lover mode in seconds. In some ways I thought that was very sexy.

Kate grabbed my hand and we went into my bedroom. I had turned music on in my room while she was on the phone and it started to play a very specific slow song.

"I love this song," Kate said, while kissing me.

The song was the one Liz and I danced to at Robert's wedding. It was my unofficial song for her. The lyrics were about a woman who thought she was flawed. No matter what her lovers would tell her, she never believed them. Then she met one man who made it his mission to show her how special she was to him and that should be enough. On his death bed, she finally realizes that the special thing they had with each other far out-weighed any kind of individual flaws she thought she might have had.

"We have to stop," I said.

"Is there something wrong," Kate asked, while looking nervous.

I sat down on my bed and began to re-button my shirt. This was all just too much for my crazies to handle. I couldn't sleep with this woman with Liz's song as a soundtrack.

"Liz is right," I said, in a serious and somber tone. "I am full of shit. I can't do this."

Kate picked up her shirt and sat down beside me.
She put her shirt back on and put her arm around me.

"Who is Liz?" Kate asked. "Is she the reason I
haven't heard from you in a while?"

"I thought she was the one," I said, rather quietly.
"We broke up. I mean she just kind of went away."

Normally, there wasn't much talking between Kate
and me. There was some polite chit chat and then we
would go right into fucking. She didn't always have a
lot of time and I was just looking for sex, but Kate and I
did talk that evening. It turned out she was a good
listener.

"You're not over her yet," Kate said. "If and when
you are, don't forget my number."

Kate gave me a kiss and left my house. It would be
the last time I'd see her. Still, she did help me realize I
wasn't ready to move on yet. Liz had changed who I
was and I didn't want to revert back to my old self.

I went back into the living room and grabbed my
wine glass. Ibaka got up out of his bed and sat down
next to me.

"Buddy, you always seem to be there when I need
you," I said, reaching down to scratch his stomach. "I
need to get my shit together before I get her back,
Ibaka."

So, I went to bed alone that evening.

132

Chapter 14

Finding Out What Truly Matters

I spent the next two weeks attempting to get my own life straight. If I was going to have any chance of getting Liz back into my life, I needed to have my own depression under control. To do this I decided to cut down on my vices.

Other girls were obviously out of the equation, so it was going to be a celibate life. I never really needed porn in my life up until this point. Readers, it turns out the Internet was created just so porn could be streamed right onto your laptop. For a couple of days I worked, ate, walked Ibaka, and searched out porn over the web.

This seemed counter productive to my mission, so I decided to go to plan B. If girls were out of the equation then I was going to need a different outlet for my sexual energy. Luckily, my job offered me a free a membership to a pretty nice gym.

I had always used the job and whomever I was dating, to provide exercise. Hitting the gym five times a week seemed like an acceptable alternative. So, I went and worked out after work each day. I did the lifting, the crunches, and I ran like the dickens on the treadmill.

Readers, I always wanted to use the word dickens in one of my stories, so there.

The only draw back to the gym was the abundance of sexy women. There is nothing hotter than a woman wearing tight work out clothes and who happens to be stretching.

"Do you mind helping me with these weights?" A random, hot female asked, as she bent over to grab a weight. "I saw you look. I don't mind."

This was a test. All I had to do was walk away. The random, hot female then walked over to me. She put her hand around my bicep and squeezed gently.

"Oh, you're in good shape," a random, hot female said, looking damn hot! "I like that."

She leaned over and I thought she was going to try and kiss me. Holy fuck did I think she was being forward. But, in retrospect I think she was really just going to whisper into my ear. Either way, I panicked and didn't stick around to find out.

"I have a pot on the stove," I said, immediately regretting every word as I high tailed back to the locker room.

I may have looked like a bit of a wussy, but I put that gym experience in the win column and I could still return and just avoid that random, hot girl.

Another thing I needed to do before I sought out Liz was to cut down on my drinking. I had been drinking way too much since she left and it was adversely affecting my mood. The gym helped because I didn't have as much time to devote toward drinking. Still, I was searching it out way too much when I was alone.

To counter wanting to drink, I decided to spend more time with the boys. George was divorced and spent most of his time held up in his home. So, he was a perfect distraction.

"We should do something after work," I said, looking at George.

"Sure, we can go grab something to eat," George said, looking very hungry.

Thank God for the gym during that point because hanging out with George generally meant eating was involved. If we weren't eating out before or after work, George was inviting me over to his place for a home cooked meal. Don't get me wrong, I was appreciative of the company, but my body couldn't handle the constant intake of meals.

Robert was my next option and I began to spend a lot of time over his house. As you can imagine, this didn't go over very well with January. The worst moment came before work one day. I had forgotten a jacket over their place and swung by to pick it up. I didn't call first and I found Robert and January in the middle of a compromising situation. Readers, it wasn't pretty at all!

"You need to stop showing up to our house unannounced!" January screamed. "We are not running a fucking inn here!"

Robert began to hang out at my place more often after that unfortunate situation. Despite some eye soars along the way, spending time with Robert, and working out every day really helped take my mind off of drinking. I was down to one glass of wine a day because I'm not a saint and I had convinced Robert to start working on January for the whereabouts of Liz.

"I will try my best," Robert said. "You will have to be nice to her and prove to my wife that you're ready. You know how hard it is to change her mind about even the small stuff."

So, my next step was to try and convince January to tell me how to find Liz. Oh, I was also going to try and be nice to her as well. I called her, sent her flowers, and even had a singing monkey serenade her with a tale of how I was doing better and would be good for Liz. To her credit January never got mad at all of my attempts, but she would always just shake her head at me.

"I don't see it just yet," January would say.

It was becoming frustrating. I was trying to change. All I wanted to do was see my Liz, but January was standing in the way.

I was starting to think maybe Liz didn't want January to tell me where to find her. To keep those thoughts at bay I picked up a lot of extra shifts at work and volunteered where ever I was needed. George and I were working a second shift one ugly evening that turned out to be anything but. We were called out to an accident on the highway and were the first to arrive at the scene. It was a stormy night and Tulsans can't drive in the elements. So, we were a little short handed that night.

"Did dispatch say how far along she is," George asked.

"No, it was an on-looker who called 911," I responded.

It was a one vehicle accident involving what turned out to be a ready to pop mom, her four year-old daughter, and their stuffed sock donkey Pierre. All three had made it through the accident with just scrapes and bruises but the mom had been driving herself to the hospital while in labor.

"How far along is she?" George asked, again. "Can we get her to a hospital?

I got up from examining her and walked over to George who was bandaging up the crying daughter. We had no time to get her into the ambulance, much less get her to an emergency room. The babies head was already beginning to crest.

"Um, have you ever done this before?" I asked. "I'm only asking, because we're not going anywhere."

George jumped right into action and headed over to the ambulance. He grabbed blankets and his gear before heading over to the mother. A squad car pulled up and I handed the daughter and Pierre over to them. There was no way I was going to miss George bring another being onto this Earth. It turned out I was going to play that part in this kid's journey onto the planet. George got on the phone with the hospital and was relaying directions over to me. We had the mom lying down in her back seat. I had my hands out like I was waiting for a football. It was both nerve racking and exhilarating at the same time.

Surprisingly, the mom was pretty calm at first given the circumstances. She did bend my finger in directions that shouldn't be possible. My finger still isn't right since that night.

"Is there a husband or somebody else you want us to call," I said, in between reassuring her.

"No, my husband is on a business trip overseas," the mom responded, while tears started to flow down her face. "Can you please give me something? Please, it just hurts so much."

There was nothing I could give her at that point. She was too far along to risk giving her drugs. So, I did everything I could think of to get her attention. George continued to relay messages to me from the hospital and in between I entertained her with jokes, a Billy Joel song, and I think I told her about my second grade play.

Readers, it was amazing being a part of something bigger than myself. In my profession it's easy to get focused on the negatives of life, but here I was helping bring something positive into the world.

"You are doing wonderful," I said. "I have a surprise for you."

George brought my laptop over to me. It happened to have a built in camera and her husband also had a camera on his computer. He called during my rendition of "Piano Man," and George set the whole thing up. The look on her face when she saw her husband; let's just say I will never forget it and it changed me.

"You look so beautiful," the dad said, over the computer from an unknown overseas location.

"I love you baby, but you did this to me and you should be here," the mom said, while stopping to snicker in between her crying.

"I will be on the first plane," the dad said.

The mom began to scream in horror. The baby was coming.

"Okay, I need you to push," I said, while a sense of calm rushed over me.

Slowly but surely the mother pushed and the baby made his way out into the world. A million different emotions flowed through my body. It was amazing to see this miracle happen in person. The mom was crying, but she was glowing with happiness at the same time. The father was also crying from thousands of miles away.

I picked the baby up and allowed the new mother to cut the cord.

"So, do you two have a name for him?" I asked.

"What do you think?" The dad said, to the mom.

"What are your two names?" The mom asked, while looking at me.

"My name is Ian and that goofy looking guy is George," I replied, with a smile.

The mom picked up her child and watched him for a second. I could see her make a decision based upon her facial expression.

"I would like you three gentleman to meet George Ian McElroy," Mrs. McElroy said. "Of course that's if it's okay with you two?"

"I would be honored," I said, smiling from ear to ear.

"Of course," George said, with a grin.

Readers, this was the kick in the ass that I needed. I had just witnessed a miracle. It was time to see if I had another miracle left in me and I was going to need it if I was going to convince January to tell me how to find Liz.

I raced home and packed an overnight bag. There was no way of knowing where I was headed so I packed a little bit of everything. I couldn't just let Ibaka have rule over the house so I grabbed one of his toys and had him hop into the back seat.

From there, I headed over to Robert and January's house, once again forgetting to call them while I was on my way. Robert was happy I stopped by, but his wife was in one of her not so happy moods.

"Do you own a phone?" She asked, sarcastically. "Did you know he was coming over?"

"I didn't know," Robert said, while shrugging his shoulders. "I might have missed the call. It was in my pocket."

I had to put a stop to this conversation quickly or January was never going to tell me. Plus, I didn't want to get Robert into any more trouble.

"January, I'm very sorry for just showing up on you," I said, trying to sound sincere. "The greatest thing just happened to me and I have to tell Liz. I mean . . . ."

Readers, holy shit! I had already known I was going to January's house to find Liz. Still, I thought it was because I had witnessed a miracle. I thought it had been a sign or something. I was right, but I had missed the point.

"Liz is my best friend," I said, thinking through each word. "Tonight I delivered a baby and all I could think about was telling Liz how wonderful it felt, but I couldn't do that and it's killing me."

"You delivered a baby?" Robert asked, with a puzzled look on his face. "How did you do that?"

So, I explained what happened and made sure to include the birds and the bee's story for Robert's sake. January stared at me the whole time with what appeared to be her version of a smile. All I could think was hopefully she wasn't waiting just for me to shut up and then was going to tell me no. Once again, I was very wrong.

"I haven't seen you with that schmuck grin on your face in a long time," January said, while getting up from her seat. "Okay, I will tell you how to find Liz."

"You will?" I asked, while flashing my grin.

"You will?" Robert repeated, while looking perplexed at her generosity for me.

January walked over to the door and grabbed her keys and purse. From there she gave Robert a peck on the cheek and opened the door.

"I get to sleep and you can drive," January said.

"What are you talking about?" I asked, completely confused.

"I'm going with you," January said, while heading out the door.

"I'm going to!" Robert exclaimed, with a grin.

"No you're not," January fired back. "You have to go into the office tomorrow."

"Good luck," Robert whispered, to me. "I have a good feeling about this trip. Things will be better in the morning."

So, I followed January out to my car and got my mind set for the mission. At least I would have gotten my mind straight if it wasn't for the diva.

"You brought your dog!" January exclaimed. "He's so not sitting on my lap."

Ibaka had wondered into my front seat while I was in the house. He was probably looking for the jerky that had fallen underneath my front seat. I glided Ibaka to the back seat and helped her majesty into the car.

"There, he won't bother you the entire trip," I said. "So, where are we headed?"

"Just drive to Oklahoma City," she said. "I will tell you when we get nearby."

Chapter 15

A Stout Love Never Dies

The trip from Tulsa to OKC was just under two hours. Still, riding in the car with January made it seem so much longer. She had previously stated she'd be asleep the whole way, but that didn't happen.

January decided to play 20 questions and she was more than happy to ask and answer whatever came out of her lips.

"So, is it me or is my husband kind of thick at times?" She asked, with a pondering look on her face.

"He can be," I said, getting cut off.

"I mean, did he really think he could come with us and skip work?" She pondered. "Honestly, I swear that man doesn't think some times."

After she discussed Robert and his shortcomings for a while, January steered the topic toward my feelings for Liz. I guess I didn't mind answering questions, but I wasn't exactly best friends with January and she liked to get personal.

"Why did you allow things to get so screwed up with you two to begin with?" She asked, seeming content with her question.

Colleen Michaels

"It wasn't that I wanted her to go," I replied. "There was just a lot happening and . . . ."

"She told me it wasn't right for you to have to take care of her," January said. "Liz thought she was holding you back."

I wanted to take care of Liz. Sure, there was the comment I made that dealing with her and my depression could be rough at times, but I didn't mean for that to be the reason she left me. Readers, Liz wasn't holding me back.

"Liz was the reason I started living again," I said, trying to hold back the melancholy in my heart. "I'm ready to do whatever it takes to get her back. I want to take care of her."

That stopped the 20 questions for a while. January just sat in her seat, deep in thought. Ibaka was also quiet, content to play with his toy on the backseat.

Before long, we hit the highway that would take us into OKC. January began to bark out orders as to where we were going. I had previously gone to college in the OKC area, but January was taking us to the outskirts of the city and I had no idea where I was going.

"Make a left at the light and pull up to those gates on the hill," January said.

I did what I was told and found myself at a rehab. It was a beautiful facility, sitting on a hill loaded with trees and a large pond. The building itself looked old, but it had character. There were green vines going up and down the walls. Half of the windows appeared to be barred while the other half were opened wide.

144

"We're here for visiting hours," January said, while having me hold down a button at the gate.

A moment later, the gates swung open and we headed into the facility. We saw a wide variety of patients as we drove around looking for a parking spot. Over by the pond seemed to be where patients would go to stare into the universe. We saw other people writing under trees and still others running around and playing kickball. Perhaps, I should come here for my next vacation.

We parked near the building and I started to get everything situated. I was worried about Ibaka, but it was a nice breezy day, so rolling down the window should keep him cool. January didn't move from her front seat position, when I went to get out of the car.

"Does she really need to be in a place like this?" I asked. "I didn't know she was this bad."

I could see tears start to come down her face. It was weird seeing January cry. I didn't know it was possible. This whole emotional side of January had certainly been weird getting used to over the course of that road trip.

"It's not my place to tell you about how she's doing," January said. "I'm not going in with you. Go on and get going."

So, I got out of the car probably looking very confused. As I went to close the door January had some parting words for me.

"Ian, she loves you very much," January said. "Just listen to her. Try not to sound or look all judgy."

There was no part of me that was going to judge Liz for getting help. Yes, I wish I had known we were heading to a rehab. I really wished I would have known she was here. Maybe, I could have helped in the process.

I walked into the facility and it didn't look at all like I was expecting. Perhaps it was the horror films I watched growing up, but I was expecting a dreary place with security doors and drug addicts walking around the halls talking to themselves. Instead, it looked like a posh hotel. The walls were painted bright colors and the patients all seemed reasonably lucid.

A very friendly female at the front desk showed me where to find Liz's room. Readers, I was really fucking nervous to see her again. January didn't tell me where I was going. What if she didn't even tell Liz I was coming to see her?

"Are there any rules I need to know about?" I asked, as sweat began to roll down by forehead. "This is my first time coming here."

"Yes, don't feed the inmates," the nurse said, with a big snicker on her face. "Look, treat her like you would if you were anywhere else. I can tell you she's excited to see you."

I guess January did tell Liz we were coming to see her. She probably wanted permission. Oh, this meant Liz really did want to see me!

A few moments later we arrived at Liz's room. The door was open and my song for her was playing. I peaked inside and the walls were bare, but painted pink. Liz always had to have pink walls in her bedroom. Her old room in my house was still painted pink from the time we stayed up and drank wine after work. That was a great night of intimacy, paint rollers, and very good wine.

Liz did have picture frames covering her dresser. I could make out photos of her mother, sister, and January. As I entered the room, I saw a photo of us. It was from our date to the Ferris wheel. A man on the street took a Polaroid of us. I couldn't believe she had saved the picture.

"Sweetie, you have company," the nurse said.

Liz put down a book she had been reading and turned around toward me. All I could do was focus on her face and wait for a reaction.

"I will be up front if either of you two need me," the nurse said, as she exited the room with a bright smile on her face.

I didn't even notice the nurse leave. All I could do was marvel at Liz as she flashed me her smile. I hadn't seen that smile in so damn long. It was everything I had remembered it to be and more. There were things I had planned on saying when I saw her. Jokes I was going to tell to help re-break the ice. Instead, I just stood there basking at Liz and her beautiful smile.

"Look, no marks!" Liz said, showing me her arms.

I continued to stand there. All I could think was what if me being there was only going to make things worse for her?

"You're allowed to enter all the way into my room," Liz said, with nervous laughter. "I promise you won't catch anything and I almost never bite."

I proceeded to shake off my momentary trance and walked into the room and had a seat in a nearby chair. Liz never took her eyes off mine.

"You're looking as handsome as ever," Liz said, with a flirty voice. "I'm happy to see you."

I spent what seemed like 10 hours trying to get my thoughts straight in my head. It wasn't the environment at all. I had just been waiting for this moment for a while and now I was just looking like a jackass.

Liz got up from her bed. She wasn't wearing some institution robe or medical gown. Instead, she was wearing jeans and a sexy blue turtle neck without any sleeves. Her arms really did look wonderful not all marked up. I was so proud of her.

Liz sat down in my lap and starred at me with a bit of a frown on her face.

"I'm sorry I didn't tell you where I was going," she said. "I needed to get away from the real world. I am Bi-Polar and this place has helped me a lot."

I brushed my hands through her hair. She had cut it short, looking for a fresh start. There was no question her new hair looked amazing.

For a moment, it seemed like nothing had changed. I had my beautiful girl on my lap and everything seemed fine with the world.

"I was embarrassed to tell you I needed to do this," she said. "I told January and my mom not to tell anybody."

"Why did that have to include me?" I asked, finally able to get words to flow out of my mouth.

"I especially wanted it to include you,' she said, as a few tears started to slowly make their way down her face. "I love you more than anything else in the entire planet. I don't think I could have handled you leaving me due to my craziness."

It always crushed me to see Liz cry. So, I used one of my fingers to wipe away her tears.

"I'm not here to judge you," I said, positioning my face just inches away from hers. "All I ever wanted was for you to be happy. The idea of leaving you never, ever crossed my mind."

Liz sat up a little bit and smiled like it was her job to keep the heavens lit brightly. She then put both her hands on my face and kissed me. Sure, she was borrowing my hands technique, but I didn't care. My baby girl was sitting on my lap and for the first time in a few months... I had felt like I was happy again.

"So, what happens now?" I asked, with a shrug.

Liz got up from my lap and reached for my hand. She proceeded to pull me out of my chair.

"Will you take a walk with me?" she asked, with a look that would have gotten me to do anything for her.

"Where are we going?" I replied, quickly.

"Stop asking so many questions," Liz said, with a smile. "Just come with me."

Liz took me back to the entrance and told the same nurse that we were going out to the pond. It had been a while since Liz and I had held hands and just walked together. It's sick how it's the little things you miss in relationships.

The weather was beautiful when we reached the pond. The water was crystal clear and you could see fish swimming around in schools.

"I'm going to stay here a little while longer," Liz said, while putting her hand over my mouth so I couldn't respond back. "I'm on the right track right now and I haven't had a bad episode in weeks. Plus, they've taught me a new diet that will help with my moods and they're teaching me tricks for remembering to take my medicine."

For just a moment all of my happiness rushed back out of my body. I was truly happy she was getting better, but I also didn't want to lose her.

"This is why we have to come up with a schedule," she added, while taking her hand off my mouth.

"What do you mean a schedule?" I asked, with probably a little bit too much disappointment in my voice.

Liz immediately picked up on that tone and reached over and kissed me again. She had her hands on both sides of my head and was making me look her straight in the eyes.

"You're not losing me," she said, very quietly. "Before you know it I will be back where I belong, sleeping next to you in our bed. You just have to give me a little more time and come up and see me as much as possible."

Liz put her head down on my shoulder after that and we just sat there starring at the fish, while I filled her in on my mission to find her. I told her about the woman at the gym, cutting down on drinking and how I helped deliver a baby. It was nice to have my best friend back and I told her that as well.

"I really do love you," she said, after I got done yammering. "I know I can be a little much to take at times, but my love for you will never change."

We spent a few more minutes by the pond discussing a visiting schedule. From there I walked her back inside and left her in the lobby standing next to the nurse. Readers, at that point, she had no idea I heard her say something to that nurse that left me wishing and brainstorming.

"I'm going to marry that handsome man one day," she said, while smiling at the nurse.

I had been hanging with Liz for what seemed like minutes, but January and Ibaka had actually been waiting for three hours. After the cloud of happiness had dissipated a little, I rushed out to the car to make sure January hadn't killed my dog.

Surprisingly, the car wasn't there when I arrived at the parking lot. I called January and she had gone to get some food. January said she'd be back in a few minutes. It was more like twenty.

Chapter 16

Wooing My Love
Back Into My Arms

The trip back to Tulsa started off quiet enough. Ibaka was asleep in the back of the car, January was reading a self-help book and once again I did the driving. It seemed peaceful to know Liz still loved me and I thought January would just let it go. Of course, I was very wrong.

"So, you were in there for a long time," January said, not even bothering to look up from her book. "Am I right in assuming things went well?"

"That would not be a wrong assumption," I replied, with a smirk.

January stopped looking at her book and turned her entire focus to me. She had spent the time I was in visiting with Liz doing her hair. So, January still had curlers in her hair as she attempted to have a serious conversation with me. She just looked so darn silly.

"Don't mind the curlers, you dork," she said, while noticing me starring at her hair. "So, tell me already. Is there going to be a happily ever after or do I need to have Robert on-call for our return home?"

"She said she still loves me," I said, as a smile beamed through my mouth. "She wants us to be together, but Liz said she still needs some time."

January turned behind her and looked at Ibaka. My dog had just farted and the aroma was making its way forward in the car. I didn't blame my Boxer, after all it had been a long day for my furry buddy.

"Your dog has been doing that all morning long," she said, with a dirty look. "I'm going to have to air out my car when we get home."

"It just means he likes you," I said, while reaching back to pet Ibaka. "He's just very comfortable in your car. You should be honored."

January rolled down her window and gave me a nasty look for my sarcasm. The topic had changed to my dog for a moment, but she quickly got us back on track.

"I knew she still liked you, you know," January said. "You two are good together."

"It took you long enough to tell me where she was at," I replied.

"Part of that was Liz not wanting you to know," she said, with a look of compassion. "Plus, you were becoming a little too out of control for my cousin. I needed to be sure you were ready to see her and find out what she had been going through for her and for you."

I had a response or two that I could say, but she was right. My drinking had been going overboard for a long while. Liz needed a man who has his shit together. In a screwed up way, January helped me make that happen.

"In case I haven't said it yet, thank you," I said, while looking January in the face and trying not to laugh from the curlers. "Today was everything I could have asked for and you made this happen."

Readers, this was one of two times I ever saw January tear up in my life time. I don't think she cried at her own wedding. The tears didn't last long as she wiped her face and blamed it on the dog's gas issues.

"Ian, you have to promise me you will take care of her," January said, once again getting back to her bossy, but apparently really caring self. "Between losing her dad, her mom being a bitch and what happened with Asshole, Liz needs a rock in her life. I really do think you're the guy for her."

It wasn't a promise I was going to be shy about making. My time away from Liz allowed me to grow up a lot. It wasn't just about the drinking or getting back into shape. I had realized that Julie wasn't the only girl I was meant to be with during my lifetime. I realized that maybe Julie wanted me to love again.

"I love Liz so very much," I said. "It has been difficult being away from her. When she returns home, I will make it my goal to never leave her side ever again.'

"That's all I needed to hear," January said, with a grin. "Just remember we had this discussion. If you go back on your word, we will throw down and I will win!"

January went back to reading her book for the rest of the trip home. I spent the time remembering every last detail of the day.

Robert was out in the drive-way when we returned back to their house. January just shook her head in amazement.

"He's like a dog waiting for his master to get home," January said, with a snort. "I suppose I do adore the guy."

I stayed over their place for a little while longer filling in Robert. After a while it was time to head home with Ibaka and formulate a schedule.

The next day arrived quickly and I was up before my alarm sounded. I sat down at my table and looked at my rough outline I had created before going to bed. I worked four 12 hour night shifts a week. That gave me three days in a row to spend with Liz. Readers, I didn't waste any time getting our relationship back on track.

I spent the four days at work each week waiting to call her as soon as my shift ended. Liz would always wait for my call in the break room. Since my shift was over early in the morning, we didn't have worry about other people at the rehab needing to use the phone.

Just talking to her on the phone helped me get through each day. I would go home, put on my pajamas, lie back in my bed, and listen to her voice. For you dirty readers out there, our conversations were almost never about sexual things. Instead, she would tell me about her day, her rehab buddies, and the daily battles of being Bi-polar. Every once in a while I think she tested me to make sure I could handle her. Liz always seemed to like my answers, so I would have to say I passed her tests with flying colors.

The best part of our conversations always happened at the end. Not because I could finally, fall asleep, but because of the four magical words we would say to each other.

"I love you dear," Liz would say, with the voice of an arch angel.

"I love you beautiful," I would say back.

Once my last shift of the week ended, I would race home to pick up Ibaka and drop him off at Robert's house for three days. He told me January was actually getting used to having the fluffy beast around.

Then I would head up to OKC to visit my girl. On the first weekend I was there we spent each day having picnics outside by the pond. Each time we had perfect weather and I would bring whatever meal I could find at the nearby grocery store.

"I really could get used to this," I said, while Liz was sprawled out in my arms and eating the last of the lasagna.

"It turns you on to watch me eat?" Liz asked, with a grin.

"Not exactly what I meant," I replied, tickling her a little bit in the process.

Liz has always had a love and hate relationship with being tickled. She had warmed me once that she had knocked a guys tooth out from him tickling her. Still, it was fun to watch her squirm a little bit and in this situation she just laughed a little. We had managed to get back to our crushing faze and it was absolutely amazing.

"When you come back home, I think we should make it a point to have a lot of these picnics," I said.

Liz looked up at me and smiled. She put her arms around my whole body and squeezed.

"Kiss me you fool," she said, in a very soft tone.

The first weekend ended with a long embrace and then a trip back to the hotel to get my suit case. It sucked going home without her. I remember debating using up all of my vacation, so I could just spend a couple of weeks up in OKC with her. I would have to, but I would need those days for something much more important.

Unfortunately, the second week didn't go by very quickly. Work was busy and I needed to take on an extra shift for a buddy. This cut into my talking with Liz time. By the end of Wednesday's shift I was chomping at the bit to see her again. As usual, Liz was able to calm my crazy down.

"I have some big news for you," she said, with a lot of enthusiasm in her voice.

"What would that be, my dear?" I responded.

"Wouldn't you like to know," she said, in an ever so sexy way. "Besides, if I tell you now it will ruin the surprise. I promise you will enjoy what I have to tell you."

The phone call was enough to get me through my last day of work. Liz was pretty fucking awesome that way. As soon as I worked my last call, it was off to see my pretty girl.

When I arrived at the rehab center the same female nurse was waiting for me in the lobby. It was as though she was playing the part of Liz's mom before a date.

"She doesn't want you to see her just yet," the nurse said. "Liz is still getting ready and she doesn't want you to ruin the surprise."

"You know, I don't really care what she's wearing," I said. "She could come out in a potato sack and she'd still be the hottest girl in any room."

"So, are those flowers in your hand for me?" The nurse asked, with a smile.

"No, but these are," I said, showing her the bouquet I had been holding behind my back. "You don't think I would forget about my favorite nurse in the whole world? After all, you do happen to have the ear of the woman I love."

The nurse accepted the flowers with a big smile on her face. Readers, it's always good to have an extra bouquet handy for the mother, sister, or aunt. In this case it was a nurse playing that roll. Either way, it worked and the nurse started to dote over me.

"My husband never gets me flowers," she said, almost sounding somber. "For what it's worth I think you're perfect for her. You treat her with such kindness."

The nurse walked over to me and gave me a hug.

"Now, don't screw this up or I will find you," she said with a smile.

"I hope you have enough flowers and hugs left for me," Liz said, with a laugh as she walked out into the lobby. "That man is already spoken for by moi."

My jaw dropped as I focused on what she was wearing. Liz had on a white summer dress with no sleeves and a big black bow around her waist. Her hair was put up like Cinderella and her face was simply glowing. I get chills from just recalling what she looked like that evening. Sometimes, the word beautiful just doesn't cover what a man is thinking.

"Absolutely amazing," I said, with a face of bewilderment. "I had no idea anybody could look this good."

Liz slipped off her small black shoes and got up on my feet. She grabbed both of my hands and put them over her heart.

"You feel that?" she asked, with a whisper.

Her heart was racing a mile a minute. It was wonderful to feel and I had completely forgotten all of this was happening in the lobby of a rehab. Needless to say, we had an audience.

"You make my heart beat like this," she said, still whispering. "You mean the world to me and I love you with all of my heart."

Liz reached up and we kissed. Readers, it was something to behold kissing Liz and then having our audience applaud like in the movies. It was a magical way to start the evening.

A minute later the moment ended and I helped Liz back into her shoes. She took her flowers and handed them to the nurse.

"Can you pretty please put these flowers in a vase for me?" Liz asked. "I don't want us to be late for our date."

From there we walked over to the OKC River Walk. Liz and I walked down to the water and took a boat ride on the canal. The night was perfect as she laid in my arms and we people watched all the way down the canal.

"They look like a happy family," Liz said, while pointing at five people waving at us.

"I bet they're in the circus," I replied, with a snicker.

"Why do you say that?" Liz asked, before hitting my shoulder with a love tap.

"I think it's quite obvious," I exclaimed. "Look at the baggy, colorful clothing the mom and dad are wearing. They're either a circus family or need to go on a reality show for the worlds worst dressers."

"I think January is right," Liz said. "You are a dork."

Liz put her head on my chest and we spent the rest of the boat ride just snuggling with each other. It was at that point I had no doubts Liz was going to be the woman I married.

It was starting to get windy out and Liz was worried about her hair. So, we went into Mickey Mantle's Steak House and had a bite to eat. Like sushi, I wasn't much of a steak fan. Still, food was the last thing on my mind. I looked around at the other women in the restaurant and then peaked at Liz. I had no idea how I had gotten so lucky.

"So, what are your feelings on having children?" Liz asked.

"Well, I was actually hoping the woman I married handles that part," I said, while laughing. "When I get married, I would love to have at least one child. Do you want to have kids one day?"

Liz stopped chewing and wiped her mouth with a napkin. She seemed to be stalling as she thought of something to say.

"I used to be worried about our, I mean my kids inheriting my Bi-Polar disease," she said. "Since I've been in rehab, they've helped silence those fears. So, yes, with the right gentleman I do want kids."

Liz and I chatted at the restaurant for the next couple of hours. I had to keep buying a different dessert, just so the restaurant didn't try and kick us out. I learned she wanted to have a daughter and how Liz really wanted to live outside of the city. Liz kept using the word "we" in her stories and then would stop and correct her pronouns. It wasn't until later, that I realized she wasn't really making a mistake by using the wrong pronoun. I was just too hard headed at the time to pick up on her hints.

The night ended back at the rehab center. We both walked over to the pond and had a seat.

"So, I think I'm ready," Liz said, while looking out at the pond.

"Is it too windy out here," I replied.

"No, silly," she said, with her sexiest smile. "I'm ready to go home with you tomorrow. I'm ready to come home to the man I love."

Chapter 17

The Day I Fell to One Knee

October has always been a peculiar weather month in Oklahoma. Some years you see really warm weather right up to Halloween. Other years, you end up wearing winter jackets over your trick-or-treat costumes.

Maybe I was bias because I was in love, but the weather that particular October seemed perfect. Liz had been home for a while and I was more than happy to tell anybody just how happy we were together and how things had been progressing pretty quickly.

Despite all of the recent changes to her life and heading back to work, Liz seemed to be taking most everything in stride. Don't get me wrong, Liz still has some bad moments or even a bad day or two for that matter. Still, she was always the one who could get her own mental stability back on track. She may have been lacking the tools or knowledge to do so in the past, but that wasn't the case anymore.

Liz was also very good about teaching me and January how to react when she might be having a bad moment. I was so proud of her. Not too long ago, she was barely able to confront her issues. Now, she had the ability to show others not to be afraid.

It was the first Thursday of October, which meant Liz worked that night and I didn't. So, I had Robert over to keep me company. We decided to go out into the garage and have a beer. Once there, Robert acted like he had something to share with me. He kept looking up and back down again. It was sort of ridiculous.

"Do you need to get something off your chest?" I asked, since he was apparently content to stay quiet.

"January and I have been curious," he said, while looking down at his beers wrapper. "Have you thought about it yet? Who am I talking to, of course you have probably thought about it once or a million times."

"Dude, what the hell are you talking about?" I asked, trying to narrow the possibilities down.

Robert smiled and continued to look at his beer wrapper. For a moment, I think he was content on letting the subject just fade away. There was no way I was going to let him get away with such silliness.

"Seriously, tell me what you're talking about?" I said.

"January and I were curious if you were going to ask her pretty soon?" He replied.

"To marry me?" I asked.

"Of course," Robert said. "I think she's the greatest thing that's ever happened to you, since Julie passed. You two make each other so fucking happy every time you're together."

Colleen Michaels

"January is really on board for this as well?" I
pondered.

"I don't think she'd ever admit this to you, but she
is astonished how well you handle and take care of
Liz," Robert said. "She didn't know you as well when
you were with Julie. I think, I mean I know, she adores
you two together."

Robert quickly punched me pretty damn hard on my
arm.

"If you ever tell my wife I told you that," Robert
said, with a serious look, followed up by a smile.

Robert went over to our garage freezer and pulled
out a Flintstones Pop-up ice cream treat. He's the only
one that eats them, but I make sure to pick up a couple
of boxes when I go out to the store.

"I am going to ask her," I said, with a smile. "But
first, there is something I really need to do."

"Buy the ring?" Robert asked, actually thinking he
was helping.

I smiled at his goofiness and then changed the
subject. There was definitely something I had to do
before I could propose to Liz. I suppose I could have
told Robert, but I didn't. In fact, to this day, only two
other people know about what I did that next morning
and I'm okay with that.

Robert left fairly early the previous night, so other
then waking up when Liz got home for a kiss, I was
fully reinvigorated from a good night's sleep. My
girlfriend would still be in bed for several more hours,
so I called Julie's parents and asked them to meet me at
the cemetery.

164

I arrived at Julie's headstone about 30 minutes later and the Johnsons had already beaten me there. Both had tears rolling down their faces as they talked to their little girl. Still, I could tell they had made peace with her passing.

Both parents saw me walking up to them and not really sure how else to break the ice, I just hugged them both like nothing else in our past mattered. Mrs. Johnson seemed a little surprised at first, but then just started shedding happy tears. Mr. Johnson tried to play it a little manlier, but that morning wasn't about holding anything back.

"Thank you so much for meeting me here," I said, while trying to control my own emotions. "I thought there were some things you should know. That you deserve to know."

"What is it Ian?" Mrs. Johnson asked. "Is everything okay? Are you okay?"

I had been struggling with how I was going to do this for quite some time. I wanted to convey to Julie's parents just how happy Liz had made me. At the same time, they needed to know I haven't and would never forget their child.

"I just don't want you two to take this the wrong way," I said.

"Are you talking about Liz?" Mr. Johnson asked, with a smile now showing on his face.

"How did you know?" I responded.

"We saw your parents at church a few weeks back," Mrs. Johnson said. "Don't be alarmed. We just wanted to make sure you were doing okay."

"Mr. and Mrs. Johnson, Liz will never make me forget about Julie," I said, as one single tear began to roll down my face.

Mr. Johnson immediately put his hand on my shoulder. He looked at me and showed a caring smile.

"You will never have to apologize to us ever again," Mr. Johnson said. "You have continued to become such a good man. We're both very proud of you."

Mrs. Johnson walked over to me and gave me a bear hug. It was nice to have both of them by my side. This morning was a long time coming and it couldn't have gone any better.

I walked them back to their car, but I wasn't ready to leave just yet. There was one other person I needed to tell. So, I went back over to Julie's grave and sat down.

It was so peaceful sitting at her grave. I don't believe in ghosts or spirits, but I do like to think your loved ones can hear you when you want them to from up in heaven.

"So, I come to you with news," I said. "I'm going to ask the woman I love to marry me."

I started to feel a little uneasy, so I stood up and walked back and forth around her headstone.

"I don't want you to think my love for you will ever be forgotten," I said, as I could no longer control my tears. "You made me happy for such a long time, but I have to let you go."

There were other people in the cemetery and I began to worry they might call the cops from witnessing me acting like a crazy person. So, I sat back down.

"Liz makes me smile every single day," I whispered. "I think I can make her happy. I know I'm willing to spend the rest of my life trying."

It occurred to me that Julie's ring was under the ground, just below my left foot. A sudden sense of panic engulfed my body as I thought about what happened the last time I was going to propose.

"I wouldn't mind a sign," I whispered, not expecting one to come. "Am I doing the right thing?"

I sat there for a minute, but nothing happened. So, I forced myself up and I was going to leave, but the weirdest thing happened. A gust of wind picked up and wrapped a flier around my leg. I almost didn't even look at the bright pink sheet of paper, but it was Liz's favorite color, so I glanced down. The flier was promoting free counseling for engaged couples. Readers, I'm not fucking with you. Now, I still haven't decided if that was Julie or a gust of luck, but I'd like to believe it was the former.

"Thank you so much," I said, while taking one last look at her headstone. "I promise I will be a wonderful husband."

Liz worked that night, so I decided to go out to eat with January and Robert. It was the weekend, so the restaurant was packed. The three of us ended up spending an hour at the bar while waiting for a table.

"This food better be worth it," January said, with a grimace.

"I promise, it will be worth it," I replied.

Eventually, the hostess took us to our table. The restaurant wasn't large, but the ambiance was amazing and I had it on good authority the chef was amazing. It helps picking restaurants when you're living with a chef.

Seeing that I was the third wheel, I volunteered to order and pay for the appetizer. I chose the sea scallops, something Liz recommended. When the food arrived, I took one bite and started to bitch.

"This is really, really bad," I said.

"I don't know," Robert replied.

"That's not even a real opinion," January said, while smacking her husband lightly.

I motioned for the server to come over to us. The service at this restaurant is impeccable, but this guy was about to have a bad day.

"Can I get you anything?" the server asked.

"Yes, I asked for the sea scallops," I said. "This is just a bunch of salt. You don't really expect me to eat this food?

"I'm so sorry," the server said, as he quickly removed my plate. "I will replace this immediately."

"No!" I said, way too loudly. "Just bring us our main courses."

The server walked away and Robert kicked my leg under the table. It fucking hurt!

"What did you do that for?" He asked. "It wasn't that bad. In fact, I thought it was pretty amazing."

"I'm sorry," I replied. "I probably overreacted. It has been a stressful day."

"Is everything okay? Robert questioned, as he started to look worried. "Have you been taking your meds? Is everything okay with you and Liz?"

Before I could answer his 20 questions, three different servers delivered our main courses. I ordered the chef's specialty of the evening. Liz told me good chefs use their nightly specialty to test new things and generally they're seasonal and better than what's on the menu.

I took one bight of the food and threw my fork down as dramatic as possible.

"Server!" I yelled, so that everybody in the downtown area could hear me.

Our server and his manager booked it over to me like the place was on fire.

"First, the appetizer was too salty," I said, trying to look very pissed off. "Now, something that is supposed to be the chef's specialty, tastes this bad. Is the chef this awful or did he or she have the night off?"

"Sir, if you could keep it down," the manager said. "I'm sorry if you don't like your food. I'm sure the chef would be more than happy to fix you something else."

"If the chef is actually here, then I want to meet said chef," I said, while standing up as though I was somebody important.

The manager and the server walked away from the table. The restaurant was quiet at first. I think the entire room was in shock. But then you could slowly but surely hear chatter coming from all around the room. My table was no different.

"What the hell is your problem?" Robert asked, while slowly focusing in on an older couple sitting at the bar. "Are those your parents?"

I turned Robert's head to the back of the restaurant, but before I could explain to Robert what was happening, an angry Liz came roaring out of the kitchen. She headed straight for the table. I stood there and watched my angel walk toward me. She was wearing her world's best chef apron and had sweat all over her forehead. Boy was she wearing her pissed off look proudly. That was until she focused in on me.

"What are you doing here?" she asked, looking very confused. "Were you the one making all of this noise?

I didn't respond right away. There was something more important I needed to ask her. So, I went down to one knee and pulled out a box from my pocket. I looked up into her big, generous blue eyes.

"Every time I see you, I know I was meant to make you happy for the rest of my life," I said.

Liz's face went from fierce to a look of shock.

"You make me a better person just by smiling at me," I continued. "I thrive to be worthy of that smile. It's the most beautiful part of my day."

On cue, Liz started to show me her smile. It lit up the room brighter than anything else inside the entire restaurant. Any second guessing I may have had now flushed completely away from my thoughts.

"Liz, you are my best friend and you are my inspiration," I continued. "I have just one more thing I need to ask of you. Beautiful, sweet, kind, and loving

Liz, will you make me the happiest man alive and marry me."

Liz just looked at me and nodded yes, over and over again. Happy tears flowed down her face.

"Of course," she said. "I would love to marry you."

I stood up and took the ring out of the box and placed it on her finger. Liz looked down at the ring and then up at my eyes. She then stood on my feet and we kissed. It was the single greatest decision of my life.

"I love you," I whispered, into her ear.

"I love you, too," she replied.

The people in the back of the restaurant were actually Liz's mom and sister. I had stopped by their place after the cemetery and urged them to be at the restaurant. Oh, yes, Robert was right about my parents being there as well. I had also clued January into my plan. Plus, I want to give a shout out to the server and the manager for going along with my plan.

It turned into a beautiful evening. Liz's manager had made previous arrangements for her to leave early, without her knowledge. Plus, January had brought a dress for Liz to wear. It really wasn't out of sorts for January to have extra clothes with her. She shopped like a Beverly Hills housewife. So, it worked well. Liz changed and we ate as a family for one evening.

"I want to propose a toast," I said. "I want to thank every one of you for being here tonight. It wouldn't have been the same without you."

Chapter 18

Celebrating Our Engagement under the Wrong Lights

George and the rest of the guys at the EMS station decided to throw Liz and me an engagement party. Halloween was right around the corner, so it was a costume party.

Liz invited January and Robert to join us, so they met us over at our house. Robert was dressed up as a pool boy. His significant other said she was a desperate house elf or something. January kept going on and on about how their costumes supposedly went together, but I didn't understand.

When the crazy couple arrived I was just putting on the last touches to my Captain Hook costume. Liz hated facial fair, so it was the one time this year I could have a mustache. I had the hat, a hook, and an eye patch as well. Of course, when Liz walked out of the bathroom, I immediately was stunned.

"You look amazing," I said, while trying to catch my breath. "I mean, wow."

Liz had gone to her stylist earlier in the day and got a pixie cut. Normally, I wasn't a massive fan of short hair. My fiancée was different. Her face just owned the hair cut. Liz was wearing a short, sexy green dress and had pixie dust on her face, arms, and legs. For one night she literally was going to sparkle prettier than any star in the sky.

"Are you ready to go, my dear?" I asked.

"Just relax my handsome bad guy," she said, while smiling. "We will get there on time."

Liz made some last second checks around the house and then we headed to the party. The four of us rode together and I volunteered to be the sober guy for the evening. I really hadn't been drinking much since Liz came back home, so it wasn't a big deal.

The party was being held at a rented out warehouse downtown. As usual, by the time we arrived the party had already started. There was a fire truck and an ambulance sitting outside that had banners congratulating us on our engagement. Everything seemed so perfect, as I escorted the prettiest looking woman at the festivities into her engagement party.

Things were jumping inside the warehouse. The place already seemed filled and I spotted George dressed up as a clown at the DJ booth. Liz and I decided to walk over and say hello. He was nothing but giggles when he saw Liz and I walking over to him.

"So, who put you in charge of the music?" I asked, while shaking George's hand.

"Don't listen to him, George," Liz replied, while giving him a hug and a kiss. "He's just jealous."

"You two are finally here!" George yelled, probably because of the music. "I'm so glad. Now I can do my thing, since I wasn't invited to the restaurant."

Readers, I didn't ask George to the restaurant that evening. It wasn't anything more than an oversight. George was hurt for a day or two. When he got over it, my second best man helped put this little shindig together. By the look of things, I owe him a whole lot!

"Ladies and gentleman, can I have your attention!" George yelled, until he realized he needed to turn the music off to be heard.

The party all got quiet and everybody looked up at the stage. George then snapped his fingers and a spot light popped up over him.

"I work better when I can see what I'm reading," George said, while sounding nervous. "Liz and Robert have made it and I wanted to take this time to say a few things. I promise it won't take too long."

Liz let go of my hand and walked over to George. She whispered something into his ear and then hurried back over to me.

"What did you tell him?" I whispered, into her ear.

Liz didn't say anything back. She just grabbed my hand, squeezed gently, and continued to look at George.

"I've worked with Ian for a while now," George said. "He has been there for me at work and in life so many times. I'm just so honored you asked me to be a part of your wedding."

George pulled out a clown's handkerchief out of his pocket. Since he couldn't get the many colors out of his pocket fast enough, his simple task of wiping the sweat off his brow became more difficult. The crowd did find it entertaining, so I suppose it worked out for him.

"Ian found himself a wonderful woman," George continued. "I have seen Liz make my partner a completely different man. I mean, I had no idea Ian even knew how to smile before you two got together."

George stopped a second because of some noise in the back of the room. Luckily, it only lasted for a few moments and then George continued.

"My brothers and sisters," George said, while now holding up a beer bottle. "To Liz and Ian; may you two have an amazing future. Never take each other for granted!"

With the toast over, George turned the music back on and Liz and I headed out to the dance floor. January and Robert beat us out there. My friend was getting down and even his wife seemed to be letting it all go on the dance floor.

Liz and I tried to enjoy each others company, but were constantly interrupted by well wishers. All of the attention seemed to get under my skin after a while, but Liz looked right past everybody else. She had this wonderful ability to make everybody else seem special, while focusing in on one person. I was a lucky fucking person because she always had her focus on me when we were together.

"You are doing wonderful," Liz said, knowing I hated large parties. "I love you very much."

"Are you having fun?" I asked.

Liz knew how to answer that question, without saying a single word. She just looked into my eyes and smiled. Everything else at the party stopped. I was just focused on her perfect lips and excited that I could kiss them every day for the rest of my life. The glitter on her face just added to how beautiful she looked.

Before I could start to dote on her out loud, a small fight started to break out. I could hear some bickering, but couldn't make out much with the music. One man was escorted out of the party, but I couldn't see who. Not knowing what was going on, I went to check it out.

Robert and a hoard of firemen where already over there when I arrived. I tried to get through to see for myself, but January stopped me.

"Where is Liz?" She asked.

"She's over by the dance floor," I replied. "What's going on out there?

"Don't worry about it," January replied. "Just go back over to Liz."

I was curious, but I figured it was a surprise or something. So I locked in on my fiancée and headed back to her, but then it happened. I heard his voice and recognized it right away. January saw me reverse course and tried to get in my way. I side stepped her and hurried out to confirm my suspicions.

When I arrived outside, Asshole was out there in his firefighter get up and he was shitty drunk. His crew was trying to get him to calm down, but all he wanted to do was yell.

"She is nothing more than a bitch hiding out in a pretty dress!" Asshole yelled. "This party is nothing but bullshit, but hey, I guess I'm the bad guy."

While stumbling for more crap to say, Asshole focused long enough to see me nearby. This was all he needed to get a second wind.

"There he is ladies and gentleman," Asshole said. "I keep telling you she's a cheater. She left me for you and she's going to fucking leave you as well."

I began to walk over to him. At least 10 people got in my way and Robert grabbed onto my arm.

"Dude, he's not worth it," Robert whispered, while trying to calm me down. "You have the girl. Ian, there is nothing left to prove."

I didn't want to admit it, but Robert was right, as usual. So, I stopped in my tracks and headed back to the party with Robert. After all, I did have Liz. She was my beautiful fiancée and I had some celebrating to do.

Unfortunately, Asshole had different plans for the evening. Before I could make it back through the crowd, Asshole had managed to get to me and he came out swinging. Similar to our first fight, his reflexes were shit due to his drinking, so I was able to duck the punch. Before somebody could stop him, he jumped on top of me, which knocked us both to the ground. I quickly rolled Asshole over and punched him once in the face. Readers, it felt so fucking awesome and I broke his nose.

Robert pulled me off of Asshole and walked me back inside the party. Liz was standing by George and January when I reappeared. She was crying all over her best friends shoulder. Yes, I had made my fiancée cry at her own engagement party. I was such a fucker that evening.

Colleen Michaels

Liz saw me come in and ran right over to me. First, she hugged me, but then she slapped me and hard!

"What the hell were you thinking going out there?" Liz asked. "You could have been hurt. Asshole is dangerous and I can't fucking lose you!

"I'm sorry," I said, while giving Liz my own hug. "I'm so sorry I scared you. I just had to make sure he wasn't going to hurt you."

"What if he had hurt you?" Liz asked. "I'm doing much better, but I need you here with me. I need my rock by my side."

With the party pretty much ruined, the four of us decided it was a good time to head home. I could tell Robert wanted to give me a piece of his mind while we were in the car, but was holding his words in due to Liz being in the vehicle as well. His wife had no such reservations.

"I can't hold my tongue anymore," January said. "The beautiful girl sitting next to you is your responsibility! The other guys can take care of shit heads like Asshole."

"January, it's okay," Liz said, while squeezing my arm. "I don't want to think about or talk about Asshole ever again."

"I'm just saying . . . ." January said. "Make sure you protect my best friend."

That was the last thing said during the car ride to their place. Robert asked us if we wanted to come in, but Liz declined for the both of us.

"I want to get my gladiator home," Liz said, with a smile. "It has been a long evening."

178

Since we were now alone in the car, I used the opportunity to try and get back on Liz's good side. She had on a brave face, but I could tell the whole incident had shaken her up pretty badly.

"I let my curiosity get the better of me," I said, while changing my focus between her and the road. "Then I heard his voice. I'm very sorry."

Liz put her tiny, but beautiful finger over my mouth. She had a way of just calming down my crazies almost instantly.

"What you did tonight was dumb and I was really mad at you," she said, while keeping her finger over my mouth. "I get that you want to protect me. You will never have to be sorry for trying to keep me safe."

I turned my head from the road back over to Liz. God, she is so beautiful.

"I love you so much," I said.

Liz looked right at me and smiled, but her beauty got overshadowed by the bright lights of an oncoming truck. I turned my attention back to the road, but it was too late. A truck had swerved into oncoming traffic and slammed right into us head first—like they were playing a game of chicken. The collision was intense and the damage even worse.

I was the first to regain consciousness at the scene. My car had been squished by the truck, so I had to work at getting myself free. The pain was horrible in my left arm and chest, but after a few minutes I did wiggle myself out and onto the pavement.

The moment I tried to stand up, my name came back to me and then everything Liz rushed its way back into my brain as well.

I dragged my beaten down body over to the passenger side door. Each step was agony and tears were flowing down my face. Readers, the crying had nothing to do with the pain. I was just expecting the worse and when I found her, that's exactly what I saw.

"Oh God, please don't do this to me," I whispered.

I wasn't able to get her out of the vehicle. Luckily, a driver had already called 911 and I could hear the sirens headed our way.

"Liz, can you hear me?" I asked, while crying. "Come on baby, open those beautiful eyes for me."

A fire truck pulled up and the crew immediately jumped into action. An ambulance arrived a short time later.

"Sir, you're badly hurt," a firefighter said. "Let us check you out and help out your friend."

I heard the firefighter talking to me, but I couldn't let go of Liz's hand. It was so small and soft and she looked so hurt.

"I'm a paramedic, so let me help," I replied, while keeping my grip of Liz's cold hand.

"Sir, you need to let us do our job," the firefighter responded.

"I don't want to," I replied. "If I let go of her hand I may lose her. I can't lose this girl."

A couple of the firefighters moved me out of the way. I would have done the same thing had I been in their shoes. Still, I felt helpless. I should have been in a lot of pain, but I didn't care about my well being. All I could think was it should have been me.

Several more fire trucks hit the scene, followed by four or five squad cars. I watched some of the crew head over to the truck. It didn't take long before I noticed something was wrong because the paramedics at the truck stopped treating the patient.

"What can you tell me?" I asked a paramedic.

"You didn't hear it from me, but the male driver is a DOA," the paramedic said.

Chapter 19

It's Never Too Late

They took us to the hospital in different ambulances. When I arrived at Tulsa Regional, my parents were already in the emergency waiting room.

"Have you heard anything?" I asked, sounding panicked. "Is she here yet? Dad, how is Liz?"

"It's going to be okay," my dad said. "You just worry about getting yourself better."

My dad could barely get that statement out. By no means is my father the type to break down and cry, but this was one of those times. When he thought I wasn't looking anymore, my dad put his arm around my mom and I could see both of them shedding tears. It broke my heart thinking they were this crushed over my minor injuries.

Readers, my injuries weren't that minor at all. It turned out I had a broken leg, a broken arm and four broken ribs. My doctors decided I needed surgery right away. I tried to protest, stating I needed to see my fiancée. Unfortunately, the doctors were fresh out of caring about what I had to say, so I was wheeled down to the operating room.

I had never been put under before, so I gave the nurse a heavy dose of questions. She was very sweet and was happy to answer most of them. There was one question she still wouldn't answer for me as the gas mask was being placed over my face.

"Can you please tell me how my fiancée is doing?" I whispered. "She was in the accident with me."

"I'll check for you and I will let you knew when you're out of surgery," she said. "Everything will be better when you wake up."

It wasn't quite Robert's line, but it had worked in the past, so I just let go. The gas took its effect on me and I went out like Tulsa's lights during a recession.

When I finally woke up it was morning. The doctors went ahead and repaired everything during one surgery. My left leg and arm both had casts. My chest felt like I had just smoked two packs of cigarettes. I was definitely in some pain.

"So, I see your awake," a nurse said. "How are you feeling?"

"I feel like I was just hit head-on by a truck," I responded, like an ass.

"I think there is something we can do about that," the nurse responded.

The nurse had put an IV in my arm and hooked it up to a machine while I was asleep. She handed me a clicker that was also hooked up to the machine.

"This is a morphine drip," the nurse said. "If you are in too much pain, just hit the clicker and the machine will help make you feel better. It will only do one dose an hour, so don't get any bright ideas."

"I'm a paramedic," I replied. "You don't have to worry about me."

I was in pain, so I immediately hit the clicker and allowed the morphine to do its job. For a few moments I was in pure bliss, but then a different kind of pain rushed through my body. I had managed to forget about her for a second and that was unacceptable.

"How is my fiancée?" I asked, with drool coming off my lip due to the drugs. "Can I see her?"

"I will definitely check for you," the nurse said, while flashing me a really fake smile. "Right now you're in no shape to see anybody."

The nurse walked over to me and checked on my pillows and sheets before leaving the room. I tried to say something before she left, but the combination of meds and a long surgery knocked me out for the count.

When I awoke my doctor was in the room and Robert was sitting in a chair over by the window. It was now dark outside, so I must have been out for quite some time.

"How is your breathing?" The doctor asked.

I tried to sit up a little bit, but was immediately told screw you by my body. It still hurt to do just about anything morphine or not.

"I'm still having a little trouble," I replied. "But it does seem to be getting better."

"Well, just try to relax as much as possible," the doctor said.

"Doc, can you tell me anything about my fiancée?" I asked. "She was in the accident with me and I can't get anybody to tell me anything."

The doctor looked over at Robert, who appeared to be trying to melt into the chair, rather then answer the question. He then looked down at his chart either because he was trying to stall or he just simply didn't know.

"Ian, I'll answer those questions for you," Robert said.

The doctor appeared to be relieved by Robert's response.

"I will be back later to check on you," the doctor said, before heading out of the room.

Robert got out of his chair and started to walk around. At no time during his stroll did he look at me. I could literally see the sweat dripping from his brow.

"So, where is January?" I asked, trying to get the conversation going.

"Oh, she's with . . . . I mean," Robert whispered.

I had only seen Robert like this one other time in my life. It was the day he came over to my house to be a friend when Julie died. Needless to say, I started to wig out.

"Robert, you better fucking tell me everything right now!" I yelled, before falling into a coughing fit.

"Dude, do you want me to get somebody?" Robert asked, while getting me a cup of ice to help with my persistent cough.

I finally stopped coughing, but that gave Robert time to stay quiet until re-enforcements could arrive. George happened to be his saving grace. He came waltzing into my room with balloons, flowers, and a pan of his leftovers. Readers, George likes to use humor and food during times of sadness.

"Hey there buddy," George said. "You are already looking better. Are you hungry?"

"I just had surgery," I replied. "I don't think they want me eating your leftover tuna casserole."

Robert wasn't shy at all about helping himself to some of the casserole. He probably figured I couldn't ask him anything if his pie hole was full. Still, I could always get answers out of George.

"Dude, did you bring me flowers?" I asked, playing coy.

"They're for Liz," George responded. "I just haven't given them to her yet because January said they weren't allowing anybody . . . ."

Robert stopped pigging out on the casserole for a second, walked over to George and told him to shut up non-verbally. Well, actually he sort of elbowed George in the arm to get him to be quiet.

"Does he not know?" George whispered, to Robert, while rubbing his arm.

I could see tears start to form in Robert's eyes while he thought about how to answer the question. Things had to be bad if neither of my two best friends could tell me what's up.

Not able to take all of the silence, I tried to sit up again to prove a point. Boy, it hurt like a son of a bitch. I began to take the IV out of my arm. Robert and George looked at me in horror and immediately rushed over to stop me.

"What the hell do you think you're doing?" George asked, with panic in his voice.

"I have been trying to get answers about Liz and nobody will tell me what the hell is going on!" I exclaimed. "It might take me a while, but I will get my crippled body over to her room one way or another!"

Yes, I was freaking the fuck out on my two best friends. I just had to, because I had no idea what was wrong with the better half of me—the way better half.

Since I had managed to loosen my IV, a couple of nurses came rushing into the room to see what the monitor beeping out of control was all about. I started to act really rude to the nurses, so George assured them he would make sure I would calm down. A nurse readjusted my IV and then they left the room.

Robert grabbed a chair and brought it over by me. He sat down and immediately put his head down and covered his face with his hands. It was the same thing Liz always did when she was nervous.

"I've been trying to find the best way to tell you," Robert said. "Frankly, I don't know how to tell you anymore bad things. You've just had too many bad things . . . ."

Robert's tears started to get the best of him. So, George decided to continue for him.

"Liz isn't doing very well," George said, his fake smile was long gone.

"Is she going to . . . . I mean . . . . I'm not going to lose her, am I?" I asked.

Before either of them could answer, January entered the room. She had obviously been crying and she

Colleen Michaels

needed a hug from her husband. Now there were four of us in the room crying and I still knew next to nothing about what was going on with Liz.

"How is she?" I asked, while looking at January.

"She loves you very much," January replied, while using a tissue to wipe off her eyes. "You have been so kind and loving to her and I hope you know that."

"Please, somebody just tell me what is wrong with Liz!" I said. "I can't take this anymore."

"Sweetie, Liz hit her head really bad in the crash," January whispered. "The doctors say she has swelling in her brain."

Every part of my body went numb. Please don't say it January.

"They put Liz in an induced coma," January continued, while tears trickled down her face.

"But she's going to be fine," I said. "I know she's going to be fine. Tell me the doctors said she's going to make it!"

January just starred at me for a few seconds. She was openly crying, so Robert went over and put his arms around her. George was stone cold still. Readers, the quiet in the room screamed volumes.

"The doctors say if the swelling shows signs of reducing then she has a chance," January whispered. "But they're also worried about . . . ."

January was unable to finish. The moment was just too sad for her. That moment was too sad for everybody.

"They're worried about possible brain damage," Robert said.

I remember feeling the need to be positive at that moment. Every body in the room was just so down.

"Have there been any signs of the swelling subsiding?" I asked.

"A little," Robert replied.

"Then there you go," I blurted out. "There will be no more negativity in this room. Liz is the strongest person I've ever met."

George unfroze and walked over and gave me a hug. It was very sudden, but I was glad to have him on my side.

"Do you remember Liz walking over to me while I was giving the toast at your party?" George asked.

"Yeah, what did she say?" I replied.

"She said you will never have to worry about Ian ever again," George said, while a couple of tears let loose. "Liz said she would be there for you no matter what. So, don't give up on her."

January tried to pull herself together as well. As for Robert, I don't think he knew how to act at that point. I also knew he'd always have my back.

"I have to see her," I said. "Can one of you help make that happen?"

Of course January was the one to take charge. She went out to the nurse's station and arranged it to where I could be wheeled to Liz's room. They waited 'till night time, so the doctors and nurses could all perform their duties on Liz and me without my presence in her room being a burden.

As they wheeled down the hallway I could see my parents and Liz's family all sitting in the waiting area.

It's funny how things tend to work out. Our families hadn't even met until the night I proposed. In fact, this was only the second time they had ever met. In those two times, they'd seen the best and worst days of our relationship.

Finally we got to Liz's room in intensive care. It was so hard to see her like that. She was lying down in the bed, her head was all bandaged up and she had tubes coming out of her nose and mouth. My beautiful princess was once again all banged up and it was because of me.

"I'll give you two some privacy," the nurse said.

I nodded to her and she left the room. That left just Liz and I lying in separate beds and me unable to protect her. Still, I was determined to stay positive. I didn't allow myself to feel anything else.

"So, our friends are worried about us," I said, while trying to faint a smile. "I told them there was no need. You're going to be fine."

It was so hard not to just try and get up. I wanted to have her in my arms, cast or not.

"You're going to get better and we're going to be talking wedding plans real soon," I continued. "I told our friends you're strong. I know you can beat anything."

I just got quiet after that. A nurse came in after a few minutes and pushed me next to Liz's bed so I could hold her hand before she took me back to my room.

"I love you very much," I said, while squeezing her hand softly. "I know you'll come back to me."

Unfortunately, my optimism started to fade when it got to day three. I had been wheeled to her room the previous two night and had been nothing but positive. Yet, there was no change in Liz. My hope was fading.

I took my laptop with me on the third night. It had been a depressing day and I wanted to show my best friend something.

"You remember that night I read your journal and we got into that big fight?" I asked. "Well I'm a hypocrite. I have a journal of my own."

I opened up my laptop and showed her my blog. Of course, I never made my blog available for anyone else to check out. The readers I spoke of were always going to be fictional.

"I started to get into a really bad place in my life because of Julie," I said. "A therapist I saw for a short time recommended I start a journal or a blog. I've written some pretty crazy things on here, but then you happened and my blog started to change."

I scrawled up and down to show Liz all of the nice things I said about her. I pretended she could seem them, but I also read each line to her. Everything just became too much for me after a while. All of my optimism had drained from my body and I just broke down crying.

"I don't know if I can make it without you," I said. "I'm so damn scared."

A few moments later it was time for the nurse to take me back to my room. I slowly positioned my body so I could hug her arm.

"Goodnight my beautiful girl," I said, quietly. "Please come back to me."

The nurse took me back to my room and I spent the night praying, hoping, and begging for a miracle.

I awoke the next morning to Robert shaking my good arm with a big grin on his face. January was right behind him, with the same grin. Before I could get my barings....

"Well, good morning," Robert declared.

"We have good news," January continued. "Liz opened her eyes an hour ago!"

"I want to see her," I replied.

January just smiled and nodded at the door. A nurse promptly entered the room with a wheel chair and Robert helped me off the bed. For a moment I got real worried I was dreaming. Then we got to Liz's room. Her mom, her sister, and my parents were already inside. Everybody had nothing but smiles on their faces.

"All right everybody, let's give these two some privacy," my dad exclaimed.

Everybody cleared the room, touching me on my shoulder and smiling as they left. Robert wheeled me over to Liz's bedside and then left as well.

"There's my handsome fiancé," Liz whispered, as she attempted to smile.

"You came back," I said, while tears started to race down my cheeks. "Don't you ever leave me."

"Of course I'm back," Liz replied. "I have a prince to marry and a new life to start. Plus, I made a promise to George that I would be by your side no matter what happens."

"I love you so much," I said. "Forever . . . . unconditionally . . . . and without doubt in my heart."

We spent all day just talking and soaking in each others company. From time-to-time we would get interrupted by doctors, family, and friends, but honestly it felt like there was nobody in the room but us and our talk of marriage, work, and starting a family.

But then George had to come in and ruin the party. Well, to be fair George was just the messenger.

"Um, Ian can I talk you alone for a second?" George asked.

I nodded yes and George wheeled me out to the hallway. He had a sad look on his face as he pointed at two cops standing by the nurse's station.

"We were able to keep them away since the accident, but they insist they need to talk to you about the crash," George said.

"They don't think we're at fault?" I asked. "The truck swerved into us!"

"No, they know it was the truck's fault," George replied. "It's just the driver passed away on scene. They just need to get your statement, so they can close out the case."

"Fine, wheel me over to them," I said. "Liz doesn't need to see them."

"There's one more thing you need to know," George exclaimed. "You both know the driver."

"Who was it?" I asked, with a sense of panic shivering down my spine.

"It was Asshole," George said, quietly. "He somehow made it behind the wheel and his blood alcohol level was off the charts. I'm so sorry."

Honestly I didn't know what to say at that point. Hell, I didn't know how to feel at that point. So, I had George wheel me over to the cops and I gave them my statement. They told me Asshole had left a suicide note. The cops said he was most likely headed to kill himself, when he saw us driving by.

I waited a few days before telling Liz. She didn't ask and I wasn't going to thrust that bad info into a healing princess' mind. When I did finally tell her, we had a good cry. Asshole had almost killed our future, but our love did overcome.

Chapter 20

Happily Ever After
With My Best Friend

Slowly but surely Liz and I recovered from our injuries. Our families got together for Christmas and we hosted a New Year's party. Before long it was the night before Valentine's Day. It was the night before I was going to marry Liz. It was my fiancée that picked Valentine's Day. She said our relationship had been a fairy tale with villains and all. Why not start happily ever after on the most romantic day of the year.

"Are you ready for tomorrow?" Liz asked, while lying in my arms in our bed.

"I've been ready for a long time," I replied, while smiling back at her.

"We've remembered everything, right?" Liz pondered.

I could tell Liz was panicking a little bit. Tomorrow was a big day for the both of us. We had 150 guests coming to our wedding. Still, with the help of January, we managed to nail down every last detail.

"Have I told you yet today how beautiful you are?" I asked.

"Yes, but I'm nervous, so feel free to dote upon me," she replied, with her million dollar smile.

"I will dote upon you plenty tomorrow when I give you my vows," I said. "I will be thinking tonight about how beautiful you will look while walking down the aisle tomorrow. I'm going to call an angel my wife."

Liz tilted her head up and kissed me gently on my neck. God she looked so beautiful. Her hair was still blond, but it was now down to her shoulders. Any signs of her injuries from the accident were now gone. My bones had also healed. I could still feel a little twinge in my rib area, but I barely gave it a second thought.

"It's time for me to go to bed," Liz said, before kissing me good night one last time.

She got up, put on her robe, and was looking for her monkey slippers.

"Where are you going?" I asked.

"It's the night before our wedding," she replied. "We should sleep in different beds."

Liz had been sleeping in my room for a while now. Her old room was pretty much just storage space. January had asked her if she wanted to spend the night over at their place and Liz declined. It was actually really sweet. Liz said she had already spent too many nights away from me. So, I figured we'd spend the night in the same bed.

"I just wanted to know you are close by," Liz said, before blowing me a kiss and leaving the room.

It was a long night sleeping alone. I did spend most of the night thinking about how beautiful she'd look. For the last two weeks Liz would stress herself out about how she'd look in her wedding dress. I always assured her she'd look wonderful. She never quite believed me though, because Liz would always remind me that I hadn't seen her in the dress yet. Readers, I didn't have to see Liz in her dress to know she was going to look beautiful. I was more worried about making sure to remember my fly was up and everything was buttoned properly.

My alarm went off around 10 the next morning. Liz had already been up and she left me a note about heading out to the hair dressers. Robert and George were going to be over any minute. So, I jumped into the shower and got ready for the day. The wedding ceremony started at 3 P.M., so there was plenty of time.

"You are looking very good on your big day," George said, as I walked out of my room.

George and Robert had let themselves into my house. They were both over on the couch watching sports and drinking coffee.

"Tell me you brought me coffee!" I said, in an 'I-just-woke-up-dude' kind of tone.

George got up and handed me a coffee. He had been losing some weight since the accident. I think Liz almost dying must have scared him a little bit. So, any chance to get up and hand something to somebody was a chance to burn some calories.

"So, what's the plan?" Robert asked.

I went over to my desk and pulled out two envelopes. I handed one to both of my best men.

Colleen Michaels

"You two have seen me through some pretty screwed up times," I said. "So, I figured you could use a break."

They both opened their envelopes and found cruise tickets.

"Liz and I both thought you could use a vacation," I said, with a laugh. "Robert, you and January are booked on a romantic Caribbean cruise. George, we got you on a singles cruise."

Robert pulled out a bottle of Patron tequila he had brought with him. He poured each of us a shot and then held up his glass.

"We have gone through a lot of hard times together," he said. "Today is not one of those days. Here's to you two making each other happy for a life time to come."

After taking our shot, we talked about sports, Jennifer Love Hewitt's hotness and then separated into different rooms to get ready. A half hour later our limo arrived and the three of us were out the door.

We arrived to the church before the ladies, but both sets of parents were already inside. When the ladies did arrive, my mother ushered them into a private room.

"You shouldn't see your bride in her dress before the wedding," my mom said. "It's horribly bad luck."

I think we've had more then enough of our share of bad luck. Still, I didn't want to risk anything, so I made sure to stay clear.

Before I knew it the ceremony was about to begin. I got into position by the priest. George's daughter was the flower girl and the first down the aisle. My parents were the first duo down the aisle, followed by Liz's mom and Uncle Brad. Robert and January made their ways down the aisle. I had Robert and George wear traditional black tuxes. Liz had January and her sister wear gorgeous pink dresses. George and Liz's sister were the last of the wedding party to come down the aisle.

Then it was time for the main event. I offered to walk her down the aisle, but she said no. Liz wanted to be able to see me as she walked down the aisle.

"I want to walk toward my future," she said.

The music began and Liz appeared from behind the doors. She was wearing a traditional white wedding gown that barely brushed across the floor. Every inch of the lace and silk made her look better than any goddess ever could. She slowly moved her way down the aisle making sure to never take her eyes off of mine. Liz was by far the most beautiful thing I've ever seen.

Everybody else in the room seemed to disappear as she reached for my hand. I was so happy as we stood there looking into each others eyes. The ceremony itself went by quickly without a dry eye in the house. Then it was time to give our vows and I went first.

"I was brought up to believe that fairy tales can come true," I began. "Specifically, I was taught about the power of true, blissful, unapologetic, happily ever after love."

I looked up at Liz and she showed me her beautiful smile. It gave me the power to continue.

"Life has a way of trying to kill the belief that love conquers all," I continued. "Along the way, I fell victim to the belief that I was never going to find my princess, my best friend, and most importantly my true love. I was going to let my romantic dreams stay where I thought they belonged; in my childhood fairy tale books that I had long since put in the attic."

I stopped for a second to catch my breath. I had rehearsed this speech like a million times, but it was still hard.

"But as soon as I stopped looking, a special girl popped into my life," I continued. "She was loud, beautiful, intelligent, silly, sexy, and best of all she seemed to want to hang out with me all of the time. In short, I gained a new best friend and the princess I grew up dreaming about in just a few weeks."

Liz's face was beaming as she hung onto every last word I said. As for me, it was both nerve racking and freeing at the same time.

"It didn't take me long to give her my heart," I said. "In return, she was my constant muse, motivating me to want to be the man I know I'm capable of being for her. Liz I will love you forever . . . . unconditionally . . . . and without doubt in my heart."

I managed to get through my vows. Now it was Liz's turn. She took a second to compose herself. Just looking at her kept taking my breath away.

"I have made a lot of wrong choices in my life," Liz said. "My mother always says I have to learn things the hard way. Now that I'm standing here today, looking at my best friend I know my mother was right."

A tear rushed down her beautiful cheek. Liz composed herself and then continued.

"I didn't believe somebody could love me the way that you do," she said. "Nobody has ever looked at me the way that you do. I feel protected, loved, and special every time I see you look at me."

Liz brought my hand close to her face.

"I promise to never lie to you," she continued. "I promise to never take us for granted. Most importantly, I promise to make you feel loved every day for the rest of your life."

We then exchanged rings and the priest told me I could kiss the bride. Of course Liz had to put her mark on the moment. She stepped out of her shoes very carefully and stood on my feet.

"You make my heart melt," Liz said, before I kissed her.

The wedding reception was at the Montgomery Museum in South Tulsa. It was the former home of some rich oil guy. The limo took Liz and me over to the reception, where we were greeted by a standing ovation by all of our friends and family when we entered. It was a lovely venue with a large dance floor, an open bar, and a DJ.

We all sat down and had a great meal. Soon, it was time for toasts and January was the first person to go.

"My name is January and I'm the best friend," she said. "I've been lucky to see this relationship bloom into something special. These two people look at each other like there is nobody else on the planet."

January stopped for a second and the audience gave a little cheer to keep her on track.

"I want you two to know that I love you both and wish you nothing but happiness," she continued. "Raise your glasses to Liz and Ian. May you two grow old together and have lots of babies."

Robert gave the other speech of the night. January said he had been practicing it for weeks.

"Ian and I have gone through a lot together over the years," Robert said. "I have never seen him as inspired as he is when he's with you. Liz, I just want to say thank you for giving my best friend a sense of peace."

Robert reached down and gave Liz a hug. Like the softy that he is, Robert wiped a tear from his eye before grabbing his champagne glass.

"Raise your glasses to this great couple," Robert said. "Liz, take care of my best friend. Ian, I always told you it was going to get better."

With the speeches over, we cut the cake and then it was time for our first dance. The DJ called us out to the dance floor. I twirled her once we got onto the floor and that was the moment it occurred to me that our relationship had come full circle. My heart first skipped a beat the first time I danced with Liz at Robert's wedding. Now, here we are at our own wedding and my heart now belongs to Liz.

"What are you thinking?" Liz asked, with a cute grin on her face.

"I'm thinking fairy tales do come true," I replied. "I love you very much my princess."

"I love you too my handsome prince," Liz said, before putting her head down on my shoulder.

Readers, it was the best day of my life. I was dancing with the best looking woman at the party. More importantly, I had found my happily ever after.

Epilogue

Robert and January started trying for kids shortly after my wedding. Robert said the house felt empty without me there all of the time. A couple of months later Liz received a call from January confirming she was expecting their first child. Readers, at one point in time the thought of January and Robert reproducing would have been sort of like a horror film. Now, I couldn't imagine a better set of parents. Lord knows they've had plenty of practice with me.

George used my groomsman present to him and met a nice woman on his singles cruise. She happened to live in the next county over and George is in love. He keeps telling me that there will be another wedding coming up soon. Liz and I have done some double dating with George and Amber. She seems like a good woman for him. He always comes to work with yummy leftovers. Amber even makes extra for him to bring for me. So, she's all right in my book.

A year after our wedding, Liz decided to do something ambitious for our anniversary. She started a website for us to manage as a couple, with the goal of helping other people with depression problems. The heart of our website is the blogs we each have. Liz talked me into finally posting all of my previous blogs.

Readers, it's funny how my blog started off as a cry for help. Along the way my tale became a love story. Now, with the help of my muse I hope my readers can take comfort in my journey. What ever your individual depression issue may be, don't allow yourself to give up hope. Sometimes, when you least expect it life has a way of sending you a miracle.

The End